This one's for Fiona, who has been putting up with my wild flights of imagination since high school, and whose friendship since our teenage years has meant a lot to me.

Norah's Ark

Victoria Williamson

NEEM TREE
PRESS

Published by Neem Tree Press Limited, 2023
Copyright © Victoria Williamson, 2023

Victoria Williamson asserts her rights under the Copyright, Designs and Patents Act 1988 to be recognised as the author of this work

1 3 5 7 9 10 8 6 4 2

Neem Tree Press Limited
95a Ridgmount Gardens, London, WC1E 7AZ
United Kingdom
info@neemtreepress.com
www.neemtreepress.com

A catalogue record for this book is available from the British Library

ISBN 978-1-911107-99-6 Paperback
ISBN 978-1-915584-00-7 Ebook

Printed and bound in Great Britain

Chapter 1

NORAH

I must be the only girl in the world who doesn't have a mum.

I don't mean like Maya Turner from my old school whose mum lives in another town cos her parents are divorced. And I don't mean like Chelsea Mackay at my new school either who says her mum's got a super-important job in New York, and that's why Chelsea lives in a foster home here in Hull. I mean I never had one to begin with. Dad says I was grown in a test tube in some space-age science lab just like in that film we saw years ago, but I don't know if I believe him or not.

Dad doesn't always tell the truth.

Last Christmas he told me Santa couldn't come cos we'd moved five times already that year and he didn't know the address of the hostel we

1

were staying at. That wasn't true. He came to the kids in the room down the hall, and they'd been living there less than a week. After Christmas Dad said the bed and breakfast we were moving to would be the best place ever, but the yukky brown carpet in our tiny room smells of pee and I can hear the people next door yelling at each other through the walls at night. We have to be out of the room by nine in the morning and we're not allowed back in before six at night, which is OK on school days, but rubbish today as it's Saturday.

Right now Dad says I can't come to the shops with him as he can't afford the bus fare for both of us. That's a lie too. Not about the money—we're so skint I can't even remember what colour a ten-pound note is—but about the shops. He took me to the park and told me to stay here till he got back, but instead of going to the bus stop he went to the betting shop at the end of the road. He'll be in there watching TV till it's time to go back to the B&B, and that means it's instant noodles and tomato sauce again for dinner tonight cos he hasn't gone to the cut-price supermarket like he said to look for out-of-date bargains.

I don't mind. I like noodles and I like the park, and best of all I like the late present Santa brought me back in January when all the posh kids in their fancy houses by the duck pond had already taken their Christmas trees down. It's a purple bike with silver stripes, and it's got five different gears and a mini cargo box on wheels that attaches to the back. Dad says it was really the local church that gave me the bike. He also says that Santa isn't real and at eleven I'm too old to believe in him, but like I say, he lies a lot.

"Is your mum here, pet?" A woman in a red coat steps onto the path in front of me, and I have to pull the brakes hard. She's been watching me ride round the pond for the last twenty minutes and frowning every time I pass her bench. I try ringing the bell, but that doesn't make her move, it just makes her frown harder and repeat, "Is your mum here?"

When I was younger I would've grinned and said, "Why, am I so cute you want to ask if you can adopt me?" But then I wasn't too clever when I was younger. Now I know better. Now I know the best thing to do is look at her all wide-eyed and frightened like she's a kidnapper and say, "Yes, she's right there." I point to a group of mothers standing round the climbing frame chatting while their kids fall off the monkey bars and get stuck in the plastic tubes. "She says I shouldn't talk to strangers. What do you want?"

It works. The woman gets all flustered, apologises, and gets out of my way. I set off again, but this time I head for the little patch of trees on the other side of the pond. Best to keep hidden for a bit. The kind of women who hang around swing parks are the type who make calls to social services, and I'm more scared of Dad getting investigated than anything. It's not his fault he lost his real job years ago and can't get another permanent one, or that the council keeps moving us to different temporary accommodation.

If social services visited our B&B, then Dad would get into trouble for stuff like having no food in the cupboards, and I might end up in foster care like Chelsea Mackay in school, even though I've got a dad who's living here instead of New York. Even if they didn't take me away from Dad, they'd probably work out the housing association folk have stuck us in the B&B way longer than the six weeks we're allowed to stay there, and they'd move us somewhere else. But this bike proves that Santa knows where to find me for once, and I want to stay for one more Christmas at least. It's April now, so that means if I want any more presents from him, I'd have to stay at the B&B for another…five…no, wait, seven…or is it…?

I stop pedalling and count on my fingers till I work out I have another eight months to go till next Christmas, then I get confused when I add another one for my late present delivery in January and have to start again. I'm not any good at counting. Dad says it's cos I've missed so much school being moved all round the place, but I think that's just to make me feel better about being stupid. I think my brain got a bit scrambled when those doctors mixed me up in that test tube. When Dad's having a good day he says I'm like the powdered milkshake they sometimes give us at the food bank: "Just add water and stir up the banana sunshine." The way he smiles when he says it, I know he's telling the truth for a change.

I try not to remember the things he says about me when he's having a bad day.

I start pedalling again, but it takes me another minute to find my rhythm. Coordination's another thing I'm not good at. Luckily I'm really small for my age, so this bike still has stabilisers, but sometimes I wish those doctors hadn't mixed my sunshine baby-mix formula quite so hard in the test tube. That girl Chelsea Mackay at my new school's a whole head taller than me, and I bet no one ever thinks she's too small to be in the park on her own or asks where her mother is, even though she's in the special class too and her counting's worse than mine.

When I get to the trees, I hide my bike behind a bush and crawl through the thick branches till I get to the big fence round the gardens of the posh houses. I've been coming here for a week now. There's a nest of baby birds inside a hollow tree and I've been bringing them bits of cereal from my breakfast and worms I dug up from the mud round the pond. Their mother must've been eaten by a fox or something, cos they were left all on their own. Without me to look after them, they would've just kept on crying for food till they got too weak and starved. It makes me so sad to think of it that my throat gets tight and my nose goes all runny, but then I remember I'm the one keeping them alive and that makes me proud instead.

I reach into my pocket for the little bag of crumbs I've brought, and then stop.

Something's wrong.

The baby birds aren't here.

I bite my lip, feeling round the empty hole in the tree and trying not to panic when I find their nest is gone. It can't have been foxes or dogs that took them. I might not be smart enough to count without my fingers, but I can work out that hungry animals wouldn't have carried away the little nest of twigs and moss along with the baby birds. It must've been a human. But what kind of person would do that?

I think of the girls at my new school—girls like Chelsea Mackay who pull my hair and call me a homeless tramp when the teachers aren't looking. I think of the boys at my old school who threw mud pies at me in the playground and laughed cos they knew I didn't have a washing machine and couldn't afford the laundrette and I'd have to wear the same dirty shirt all week. That makes me bite my lip harder. If any of them found the baby birds, they wouldn't feed them and take care of them like me. They'd probably do mean things to them just for the fun of it. That's what happens when you don't have a mum to look after you.

Just then, behind the fence, I hear the sound of twigs snapping. There's a little hole where a knot of wood fell out, and I put my eye to it, peering into the fairyland beyond. The home at the end of the garden is like a palace. It has fancy windows like a gingerbread house, with arches and chimneys and roses growing round the door. The garden's full of colourful spring flowers, and there's a fishpond and patio with a barbecue, and even better, a set of swings and slide that's just as good as the ones in the park. Ever since I found the birds' nest, I've been looking through the magic peephole and imagining what it would be like to live in that other world.

But the house and the flowers aren't what I'm looking at today.

There's a boy in the garden, and he's got my nest full of baby birds.

His dark skin makes me think of our school teacher, Mr Simmond, but our teacher's got cornrow braids, not cropped hair like him. The boy's much taller than me, and he's dead chubby cos he probably gets to stuff his face on as much cake and ice cream and barbecued burgers as he wants in that posh palace of his. He's carrying the birds to the ladder of his treehouse. He's got a mini castle up there in the branches, an amazing adventure playground all of his very own, and he's going to hide my birds away where I can't ever see them.

I want to shout at him that they're my birds, that he has no right to take them away from me. Apart from Dad, they're all I've got to talk to. I'd even trade my bike to get those birds back, and I love this bike more than anything. But the boy wouldn't want my bike. He doesn't need it. He has everything he could ever want, and it's still not enough for him. He's like that rich man in the story I heard in Sunday school last week, who had a field full of sheep, but took the little lamb away from his neighbour even though it was all the poor man had. I want to tell the boy the story, but I don't. I'm scared he'll just laugh at me and then tell his parents there's a smelly girl in unwashed clothes snooping around their fancy garden.

So instead I pick up my bike and cycle away, pretending that the birds don't matter to me and that it's really just the wind stinging my eyes and making it hard for me to see.

Chapter 2

ADAM

Finding the baby birds is the best thing that's happened to me in months.

The next-door neighbour's cat got their parents. She's a vicious ginger monster that pounces on anything that moves, and she's been terrorising the local birds for weeks. She caught the mother robin down by our fishpond when she was taking a drink, and the father robin a day later when I left some berries out for him on the bird table. I thought their chicks had probably died, and that made me feel terrible. I've spent enough time in hospital to never want to see death ever again. But today I heard them cheeping in the trees behind the fence in the same place the mother built her nest last year, so I knew they were her chicks. The only way to keep them safe from the prowling cat is to put the nest somewhere out of reach till they're ready to fly.

It was a tricky rescue operation, seeing as I'm not allowed out of the garden.

Luckily it's Saturday, so my home tutor isn't here making me do maths and essays. My father's at work as usual, and my mother's got her rubber gloves and disinfectant out and is scrubbing out both bathrooms as she doesn't think our cleaner's done a good enough job. That means nobody's watching me for once. I found the key for the back gate in the kitchen drawer and sneaked out to the trees behind the fence. I wish I could've gone right into the park, but I'm not brave enough for that. I'm not a coward or anything—if there's one thing being in and out of hospital for the last couple of years has taught me is that I'm tougher than I thought I was.

There's only one thing in the whole world that scares me, and that's my parents.

When I was little, I thought my parents were superheroes. My mother ran an insurance company that employed hundreds of people and that meant she didn't have much time to spend with me, but she made sure we had a few hours together for a picnic or a long walk at the weekend. Even though my father's law firm made him fly all round the world to meet with clients, he still had dinner with me every night when he was home and read me bedtime stories after he'd done his evening paperwork. That was before I got sick.

The sickness changed everything.

We left our old life behind and moved to Hull so I could be closer to a clinic offering a new type of treatment. Instead of picnics with my mother there were visits to doctors with white coats and serious faces. Instead of mealtimes with my father there were tubes attached to my body pumping chemicals that made me vomit. Instead of bedtime stories there was the endless smell of disinfectant in my hospital ward, and the hushed voices of nurses telling the other dying kids to go to sleep. Even that wasn't what frightened me. It was the look on my parents' faces every time they visited that made my heart pound. My mother used to be so calm and in control all the time. I'll never forget the panic in her eyes whenever I threw up or the numbers went down on the machine I was attached to. My father used to be so strong and certain about everything. I'll never forget the way he wrung his hands helplessly and looked so lost every time the doctors talked to him about me.

Those memories stopped me going further than the line of the fence when I sneaked out of the garden gate for the birds, same as they always do when I dream of escaping. The thought of ever seeing that fear in my parents' eyes again keeps me from leaving the garden, even though I've been much better for months and the doctors say I can go back to school. I don't argue with my mother when she says I need to have a private tutor to teach me at home now and that it isn't safe for me to go out and play with other kids. I don't beg my father to let me go back to the swimming lessons I loved more than anything, even though I hate being so overweight from all the medication and my biggest dream in life is to be an Olympic swimmer. I just do what I'm told, as that's the only way to keep the terrible fear out of my parents' eyes.

My old life is gone. I have no friends, no school, and my mother won't even let me have a pet to talk to as she's scared I'll catch germs from it.

That's why these birds are so important to me, and that's why I carried them up to the treehouse like I'd just found the most precious treasure in all the world. My father got builders to put the treehouse and swings up when I got back from my final stay in hospital. He said it was a coming-home present, but I'm not a little kid anymore, and I'm pretty smart. I can work out all by myself that it was an excuse to stop me pestering my mother to let me go to the park or visit the beach like I used to before I got sick.

Our house is full of excuses.

I've got an expensive computer and video game system to stop me asking if I can go out and make real friends. I've got an entire library of books and films to stop me asking if I can see the real world for myself. And don't even get me started about my private tutor who's there to stop me going to a real school like normal kids. It's nearly the Easter holidays and then there'll only be one term left of Year Six—after summer it'll be time for secondary school. It's more than long enough for my mother to come up with so many new excuses to keep me at home that I'll never ever escape this prison.

But these little birds can escape, at least. I set the nest down on the bottom shelf of my treehouse bookcase that's full of comics and adventure stories and take a closer look at them. There's four of them, all speckled brown and chirping for food. Luckily they're fledglings only a few days from being ready to fly, or I'd have trouble feeding them. Younger chicks need worms and insects, and as I'm not allowed anywhere near soil or mud, I'd have a hard time hiding the dirt under my fingernails if I had to dig anything up.

I pull out the little bag of berries, seeds and grated cheese I made up in the kitchen when no one was looking and set to work feeding the hungry chicks. They don't sound grateful for the food, it just makes them cheep louder, but when they're full and finally settle down, they snuggle up against each other and go to sleep. When they wake up, they can hop about the treehouse and practise flapping their wings without that cat being able to get them. It makes me smile to think of them tap dancing about all safe and warm up here while the cat can only shake her fist at them through the locked door like something out of a cartoon.

I'm not a big fan of cats—I'm more of a dog person.

We used to have a dog called Benjy when I was very little, but that was before I got sick and everything changed. Now every time I ask about having a pet, my mother brings back another stuffed animal from the big toy store in the middle of Hull. I wish she wouldn't. I'm not a baby anymore, and anyway it makes me feel like I'm still sick with everyone buying me "get well soon" gifts. I don't say that to her, though. I wouldn't like the way it would make her eyes go all sad and disappointed.

I roll up the rug and scatter the rest of the food across the varnished floorboards, making sure to put some of it a bit higher up on boxes and shelves. That'll encourage the birds to flap around and use their wings. I'm not sure what I'll do when they're ready to fly for real in a week or so—their parents didn't escape from the tomcat, and they could fly. The best thing would be to take them somewhere else and let them go, but how can I do that when I can't leave the garden?

I tie the curtain back from the window to make sure the birds get enough sunshine, and I look out across the park. It's not the swings full of kids, the families having picnics on the grass or the people walking their dogs that makes my chest ache when I think of what I've lost, it's the duck pond. The sun shimmers on the wide stretch of water in exactly the same way the lights at the swimming centre used to glitter on the surface of the pool, inviting me in, reminding me of my lost Olympic dreams.

I look down at my chubby legs and round belly that ballooned in hospital because of all the drugs I had to take, and feel miserable. Even if a miracle happened and I could convince my mother that it was safe for me to go swimming again like the doctors said, I don't know if I could ever be fit and strong like I used to be. Maybe I should stop dreaming of the impossible and just accept that this is my life now.

I'm just turning away to look at the birds again, when something in the distance catches my eye. There's a flash of silver on the path near the pond, as bright as an electric spark. I press my face to the glass, peering through the tree branches beyond the fence. The silver comes into view again further on, and now I can see it's the paint on a bike being ridden by a girl who doesn't look big enough to be out in the park on her own. I can't see her face, but the wind is whipping her black hair behind her like a horse's mane, and it makes me think of the TV show I watched the other week about wild mustangs running across the prairies in the American west. She looks so like them— wild and free without any grown-ups hovering around her telling her what to do—that for a minute I feel almost mad with envy.

"Adam? It's time to come in, it's getting cold out there." My mother's worried voice carries all the way down the garden to the treehouse.

Cold? I roll my eyes. The afternoon sun is shining down, and the daffodils are in full bloom. I've got a jacket on over my jumper, and two pairs of socks on just in case.

"Adam? Where are you?"

There's a new note of panic in my mother's voice that makes my heart lurch. I forget all about the girl on the bike and thoughts of freedom, and run back to the house before the fear can turn the sunshine into shadow and make my mother's eyes cold and dark.

Chapter 3

NORAH

When Dad picks me up at the park at half five I can tell straight off that he's not had a good day. His shoulders are hunched and his hands are stuffed deep in his pockets like he's trying to hide the fact there's nothing in them. The smile he gives me stops halfway up his face and doesn't reach his eyes. "Hi, Norah," he sighs. "How was your day?"

Norah. That's another bad sign. He calls me that when he's feeling sad. When his pockets are full and his smile is real he calls me "Sunny" instead, like my favourite banana-sunshine milkshake. The sun's lost its warmth, and it's chilly in the park. Dad's hands are cold as ice when he ruffles my hair.

"It was fine," I shrug. I want to give him a big grin to warm him up, but I'm too sad about the baby birds, so I settle for rubbing his hands instead. "I played on the swings and made a secret den out of branches." I don't mention the injured mouse that I've got in my bike box. Now's not the time to tell him there's another mouth to feed.

"That's good, pet. It's a long time to be out on your own. Tomorrow will be better. You can see your friends at Riverbank Hall, and that'll be more fun, eh?"

This time I manage a smile. We go to church every Sunday, and Dad sits at the back listening to the minister while I go to the Sunday school in the big hall to sing songs and colour in pictures from the Bible. I don't think Dad believes in God. I'm not sure if I do either, but after church there's a free coffee club and we get to have as much cake and biscuits as we like, and that feels just like Heaven to me.

"Come on, the wind's getting cold. Let's go back and get something hot in your belly for dinner."

We head back to the bed and breakfast in silence; him trudging along with his head down and me pedalling like mad to keep up with his long legs. It's not an awkward silence, though, the way it is with the kids in school who don't want to talk to me cos they think being poor is a disease you can catch. Dad and me are best friends, and we can have a whole conversation with just a smile or a hug. I know exactly how he's feeling without him saying a single word.

It's six o'clock exactly when we get to the B&B, and that means we can finally go back in. They probably had different rules years ago for families on holiday and proper guests, but now that it's mostly all homeless people like us they don't need to treat us like we matter. The paint around the windows is all chipped and the wallpaper's peeling off, so maybe they don't think we're worth fixing the place up for either.

The manager scowls at Dad when she sees him carrying my bike up the stairs, but it's not like we can leave it out in the yard, is it? Anything that isn't fixed to the ground with a ten-foot nail gets nicked around here, and my bike's the most expensive thing we own. Dad dumps it in a corner of our cluttered room and sets to work getting the food ready while I try to rub the grease off our plates with a tissue. I should probably take them to the bathroom at the end of the hall to wash them, but I can hear the manager's husband shouting at the woman next door about washing her kids' clothes in the bath, so now probably isn't a good time. Luckily there's still water in the electric kettle from this morning, so I don't need to risk getting into trouble carrying that out. We're not supposed to have any food in our room, but since nearly everyone here is homeless, the manager turns a blind eye to kettles and toasters as long as we don't make it too obvious. She threw someone out last week for having a microwave, though, so we have to be careful not to break rules like that.

I was wrong about dinner—it's not instant noodles, but beans on toast. Dad remembered to leave a can on the radiator before we went out this morning, so it's almost warm by now. I'm not sure the heating's been on, as it's mostly freezing here at night, but at least the sun's done a good job of heating the metal can up through the grubby window. The room's tiny and we don't have a table, so I put the plates of toast on the bed and Dad spoons lukewarm beans onto them and hands one back to me. He's given me the biggest one again, but he won't swap.

"This one's plenty, pet. You eat that up while it's still warm."

"But you didn't have any breakfast," I frown, feeling guilty at how quickly I'm gobbling up the beans. "Aren't you hungry?"

"Nah. My pal, Ed, got me a sandwich at lunch, so I've had plenty today."

That makes me frown harder. I don't like Ed, and I don't like it when Dad lies to me. Ed's a mean little toad who wouldn't share a parachute with his own mother if they were pushed out of a plane together. There's no way he'd fork out a whole pound to get Dad a roll from the bakery. Ed's a bad influence. Dad only goes to the betting shop when Ed's around, and then he always has a bad day. I don't say that, though, or tell Dad that I know he was down at the bookies instead of looking for bargains at the shops like he said. It would just make him feel bad. *It's not like Dad gambles or anything*, I remind myself. *He just goes there to watch TV cos we don't have one in our room.*

I want to believe that even more than I want to believe it really was Santa who brought me my bike.

Dad leans back on the bed and unfolds the newspaper he picked up at the bookies when he was pretending to go to the shops. I don't know why he bothers bringing them back— he's not any good at reading, and that's why it's so hard for him to find a proper job. I hide my toast crusts in my pocket and try to sneak the mouse I found in the park into my old hamster cage when Dad isn't looking, but he hears me fiddling with the bike box and looks up.

"What's that you've got there?"

"Nothing, just tidying up."

"Norah!" Dad sees the mouse before I can slip it back in the box, and he rolls his eyes. "What have I told you about bringing stray animals back here? If the Crabbits downstairs know you've got a pet in here, they'll kick us out." That's not the real name of the manager and her husband, but it suits them better than "the Babbits".

"But *Dad*! This little mouse has a bad foot, and she's limping. She'll get eaten if I leave her outside cos she can't run away." I know I shouldn't ask for stuff, especially if it either costs money or might get us into trouble, but when it comes to animals that need me to look after them, I just can't help it. "It's only for a few days—just till her foot's better. I'll hide her cage under your newspaper so no one will see her."

"It's bad enough you bringing insects in here and turning this place into a bughouse," Dad grumbles, glancing over at the window where my pet spider, Boris, is hiding in the corner waiting for flies. Boris is a big house spider I rescued from our last hostel. I found him in a dusty web under the bed six months ago, and now he's the only friend I have left. If I hadn't brought him with me to the B&B

24

he would've been hoovered up by the hostel manager when we left.

"*Please* Dad?" I beg.

"Just for a few days, then," Dad sighs. "But if he makes any noise he's going straight out, OK?"

"Thanks, Dad."

I pop the mouse into my hamster cage quickly before he can change his mind. My hamster died last month. I had her three whole years, which is ancient for hamsters, but I was still really sad when I had to bury Mrs Nibbles in the park. Dad bought her for me just before he lost his old job and we had to move away from our proper house cos we couldn't pay for it anymore. He let me bring Mrs Nibbles to every new place we moved to, which was really nice of him seeing how much trouble we could've been in if anyone found out I was keeping a pet. We couldn't afford real hamster food from the pet store or anything, but she seemed to do OK with bits of my breakfast toast and the cake crumbs I scrounged from the bins behind the bakery. Sometimes I think my hamster was better fed than my dad, and that makes me feel really bad.

"Can I get you another bit of toast, Dad?" I ask, standing on a stool and checking in the cupboard to see what's left till he gets his benefits money next Friday. We've finished all the bread, though, and all we've got is a can of spaghetti hoops, a packet of instant noodles and a dribble of tomato sauce at the bottom of the bottle. We'll have to go to the foodbank this week to see us through, and I know how much Dad hates that.

"I'm fine, pet. You go out and play and let me have a nap." Dad looks really tired, like eating a bit of toast and a few mouthfuls of beans was a big effort. I pull his shoes off for him and fetch a blanket, and he gives me a sleepy smile and closes his eyes. I've used up all the paper in my colouring books and my Play-Doh's gone hard, so I head out into the corridor to see if any of the other kids want to play. There's three kids squashed into the room next door, but they're all too little and their mother's always shouting, so I avoid that door and knock at the one near the end. Kim sticks her head out to see who's there, and a minute later she comes out with her little brother, Ollie, for a game of tag.

We run up and down the corridors for a while, but it's not much fun as there's no room, and anyway Kim is thirteen and Ollie's only seven, so it's not really a fair game. Then Mr Crabbit comes marching up the stairs to tell us to cut it out as we're making too much noise, and Kim and Ollie go back inside their room cos they're scared of him. Their mum's sick and their dad doesn't like anyone else in the room, so I can't go and play with them in there.

I mooch about the corridors for a bit, looking for something to do, but no one else is coming out to play. Everyone's afraid of getting thrown out for causing trouble, like that lady with her microwave last week, so they're keeping their kids inside. I slump down on the floor and pull out the crumpled piece of paper I always keep in my pocket. This is my special list. It's all the things I want in life to make me happy. We were supposed to write it for homework a few months ago, but I didn't hand it in. I was scared the teacher would read our lists out in class and Chelsea Mackay and her gang would laugh at me. My spelling's really bad, but my list goes like this:

1. Go to a skool were Im not bullayed

My first school I went to when we rented a proper house was great, but when we got kicked out and moved to the hostel I had to change schools cos it was too far to travel. My next school was terrible, but the one I'm at now is even worse as it has Chelsea Mackay in it.

2· Dad gets a job so hes hapy and we hav munay and a propr howse

Dad sometimes gets jobs, and that makes him really happy for a bit, but they never last more than a couple of months. Then he's back on benefits, and then we don't have enough money to pay the homeless hostel rent, never mind get a real house to live in. But if we don't get a home of our own, I'm never going to get the next thing on my list:

3· Get a reel pet, maybay a dog or a cat or a rabit

Having a hamster was nice, but it's not the same as a pet that comes when you call it and is all happy to see you when you come back from school. Mrs Nibbles didn't do anything I asked her to do, even though I trained her for hours and hours. Maybe if I had a proper pet I wouldn't need the last thing on my list, the one I know would make Chelsea Mackay laugh at me if the teacher read it out:

4· Get a frend

I used to have fun with the girls in my first school, but that was years ago, and I don't have a phone or a computer to keep in touch with them. They probably don't remember me now anyway. I meet new people in every place we move to, but we never stay long, and then I have to leave them behind and start again. Kim and Ollie at this B&B are nice, but I know either their family or me and Dad will have to go somewhere else without any warning. How can you be real friends with someone you might not see again tomorrow?

The list doesn't seem like a lot to ask, but I might as well wish for the moon.

I crumple it back up and stick it in my pocket. I'm so bored I could scream. I don't want to go and disturb Dad just yet, so I try to break my wall handstand record instead. I get halfway there, but then I get a fright when another door opens and a man yells, "What the hell are you doing?"

Even upside down, Marty Mad Dog looks like the meanest thing I've ever seen. That's not his real name, but that's what all the kids call him. I was so busy doing handstands against the wall I forgot his room was the one right at the end of the corridor. I scramble upright again and back away quickly.

"Sorry!"

"Get out of here or you will be." Before he slams his door, I catch a glimpse of two beady eyes in a thin face that looks so hungry he'd probably eat me if I let him catch hold of me. It's not all families in here. There's also people who smell like they haven't washed in years and who are all twitchy and snappy like dogs that've gone half wild. I try to stay away from them as much as I can.

There's nothing for it, I just have to go back to my room. I try to sneak in without waking Dad, but he rolls over and looks up when I open the door. At first I think he's going to say something grumpy, but then he holds open the blanket, and I skip over and snuggle up next to him. He used to be big and strong when he worked as a builder, but ever since he lost his job, he's been getting thinner. Now when I hug him he feels like skin and bones, and I'm scared to let go in case he doesn't have any muscles left to hold him together and he just falls apart.

"Are you alright, pet? Did you get enough to eat for dinner?"

"I'm full up," I tell him, ignoring the rumbling in my belly that's already started even though it's not dark outside yet.

"And you weren't too bored today at the park all by yourself?"

"I had lots to do. It was fun." I close my mouth before I can tell him about my baby birds and the rich prince who carried them away to his castle.

"But you looked really sad when I picked you up." Dad's stroking my hair and looking at me with his eyes full of worry. He might not be any good at reading the newspaper, but he can read me just fine. "Is everything going OK at school?"

I try not to think about Chelsea pulling my hair and the boys who threw mud pies, and all the other things I've never told Dad about. If I let the hurt show on my face, Dad would get mad that kids were being mean to me and march up to the school to sort it all out. But then he'd get really sad and feel like he wasn't looking after me right, and seeing him sit all hunched up with his head in his hands would make me feel way worse than a hundred Chelsea Mackays and all the nasty boys I've ever met put together.

I put on my biggest banana-sunshine smile and nod. "Everything's great, Dad, really."

Dad isn't the only one who doesn't always tell the truth.

Chapter 4

ADAM

We're having roast chicken for dinner tonight, and homemade chocolate cake for dessert. I say "we", but I really mean me and my mother. My father doesn't eat dinner with me anymore, he's too busy. He's in the study right now typing away at his computer even though it's seven o'clock on a Saturday night and he hasn't had a day off since I left the hospital. Maybe he's trying to make up for all the time he had to waste sitting at my bedside when I was sick, and pay for all the healthcare bills.

The doctors said leukaemia is a type of cancer that anyone can get, and that I shouldn't ever blame myself for being sick. I can't help wondering if my father does blame me. He's so busy working he's hardly home anymore, and even when he's here he spends all of his time in the study and barely speaks to me. My mother's the opposite. She never used to be home in time for dinner, but she gave up work to look after me when we moved to Hull so I could be nearer the private hospital. Now she spends all of her time in the house cooking and cleaning, which is a bit pointless as we still have a cleaner coming twice a week who used to do most of the cooking for us too. I don't know why my mother won't go back to work— she used to love her job.

Maybe that's another thing I've ruined by being ill.

"Let me get that." My mother takes my knife and fork and cuts up my chicken into tiny pieces for me like I'm three years old. I bite my tongue and count to twenty under my breath so I don't snap at her and say something that'll make her look sad and disappointed. She spent over two hours in the kitchen making dinner and another two hours baking the cake this morning, so I don't want to spoil this for her too. When she starts cutting my boiled carrots I can't help opening my mouth, though.

"Just leave it, Mum. I can do it myself."

My mother stops and blinks at me, and there it is: that sad look in her eyes that says she was only trying to help and I've been mean to her. I try to make it up to her by taking a bite of her cooking and say, "Mm, this is really good," and that at least makes her smile. I know she's finding it hard getting used to me being well again and not needing everything done for me. But even people in prison are allowed to eat their own food without some guard coming over and spoon feeding them. If being sick wasn't my fault, then how come my mother acts like I can't even be trusted to use a knife and fork on my own anymore?

"So what did you get up to today, Adam?" she asks, watching to make sure I chew my chicken carefully before swallowing. I got so weak when I was in hospital, that one time I nearly choked on a mouthful of ham sandwich and that scared her half to death. "Did you get all of your homework done?"

"Yes, it's all finished. I just need to type up an essay for Monday," I say without much enthusiasm. My tutor's really good and we study lots of interesting things, but I miss going to school and having friends. I know I shouldn't bring it up again, but I can't help myself. "The doctors said I'm well enough to start school again. I'd really like to go to the local one after the Easter holidays so I can get to know some people there before secondary school."

"It's too soon to be thinking about school, Adam," my mother says without looking up from her mashed potatoes. I much prefer roast potatoes, but I couldn't eat much solid food when I was in hospital, and she still spends hours boiling everything into a soft mush even though I'm better. No wonder my father doesn't want to eat dinner with me anymore.

"But there's only one more week of school left, then two weeks off at Easter. That'll give me three whole weeks to let the new school know I'm starting and get a uniform."

"I mean it's too soon for you to catch up on everything you've missed," my mother says quickly. She looks up now, her smile too bright and fake. "It's been two years, Adam. I don't want you to feel bad that you've fallen behind your friends."

What friends? I want to snap, but I bite my tongue again before that comes out. It's hard keeping in touch with people when you've been in and out of hospital for what seems like forever. Everyone I used to know at my old school has already moved on without me. I'm not ready to give up yet, though.

"I've been studying really hard for the last six months. My tutor says I'm already ahead of where the other kids in Year Six are now." I say it quietly, carefully, the way you talk to an unpredictable dog when you're not sure if it'll lick you or bite you.

"Well, there you go then!" My mother's smile turns triumphant. "You don't want to be bored learning things you already know, do you? That would be a waste of your talent."

I just can't win. I know I should just let it be, but I want to be normal kid with a normal life again so badly I can barely swallow my chicken even though I'm healthy now. "But it's not just about the schoolwork!" I plough right on, ignoring the big warning lights flashing in my mother's eyes. "It's about having friends, and playing football after school, and going to the park, and—"

"That's enough, Adam!" My mother's voice comes out not much louder than a whisper. It's way worse than hearing her shout. It's like her throat's all choked up with chicken too and she can't breathe. "Just eat your dinner. We'll talk about it after the summer holidays, alright?"

But we won't, though. Just like we won't talk about the fact that I'm not even allowed out of the house to go to the shops in case I catch germs and get sick, or the fact that apart from the cleaner and my tutor, no one's allowed to visit us anymore in case they've got a cold or a cough and they pass it on to me. There was a time when my immune system wasn't working and that could be dangerous, but it was so long ago now it seems like another lifetime. My mother just doesn't seem to get the fact that things are different now. I don't know if my father gets it or not. It feels like a hundred years since I actually had a proper conversation with him.

The rest of dinner is awkward. Not because there's silence—it'd be much more comfortable if there was—but because my mother fills every little pause with endless nervous chatter about the food or what she's thinking of cooking for dinner tomorrow. She keeps offering me things—butter for my mash, more orange juice, extra peas—until my head's buzzing and I'm longing to be on my own. I don't know how it's possible to say so much and say so little all at the same time.

I do my best to eat the cake my mother spent so long making for me, but I'm desperate to get away from the table and can't manage more than a couple of mouthfuls.

"I'm full. Can I go and type up that essay now?"

"Oh." My mother's face falls. "Don't you like the cake?"

"It's really good," I say quickly. "I'll finish it later."

"Well, how about we watch a film together? Or we could have a game of Monopoly? Or how about—"

"Maybe later. Thanks, Mum." I'm itching to get away to my own room so badly it's like my feet are on fire. I race to the kitchen with my plate then bolt up the stairs before she can suggest anything else for us to do. I can hear my father typing on his computer as I pass the study, but I don't go in to see if he'd like to watch a film or play Monopoly later. I already know what the answer will be.

I flop down on my bed and close my eyes, heaving a sigh of relief.

I want to go out to check on the baby robins, but I can't as my mother will fuss about me going into the garden in the evening even though it's not cold. I don't want her to find out about the birds. She'd be upset if she thought I was going near animals that might have germs.

I want to talk to someone who isn't my mother, but I've lost touch with everyone I used to know, and I can't make any new friends since I can't go to school.

I want to look up information on the Internet about caring for fledgling birds so I know what to do when they're ready to fly, but I can't even seem to find the energy for that either. What's the point? The only place I can let them go is the garden as I'm not allowed to go anywhere else, and then the ginger cat will get them anyway.

Everything is just so pointless.

The last of the sun is shining through my window and reflecting off the swimming trophy I won at the local schools' competition years ago, before I got sick. The doctors said it would be good for me to keep swimming to build my strength back up, but my mother says there's too many germs in the swimming pool. The sunlight on the silver cup reminds me of the girl I saw today riding on her bike with the wind in her hair. I bet no one ever keeps her locked indoors or worries about her catching a stupid cold. I bet she can do whatever she wants.

I heave another big sigh, then unscrew the top of one of my bedposts, fishing inside the hollow tube for the bit of paper I keep there. There's nowhere else in the house I can keep anything secret. Our cleaner just hoovers and dusts the surfaces, but Mum goes through all of my drawers and wardrobe once a week doing a big clean, so if I tried keeping anything in there she'd find it. I don't want her to see this. I'm pretty sure it would make her sad. It's a list of all of the things I want now that I'm getting better again. The doctors asked me to write one when I was sick—I think it was supposed to help me focus on all the things I had to look forward to and help me get through my treatment. I threw that list away, though. It was full of stupid stuff like "Get well so I can play computer games and eat chocolate cake without being sick". Now that I can do those things, they just don't seem important anymore.

I unfold my hidden list and take another look at all the things that really matter:

1. Go back to school
2. Convince my mother to go back to work
3. Get a pet
4. Make some friends to have fun with
5. Fix my parents

Come to think of it, number five should probably be the first thing on the list, as it's the most important one. If I could just find a way to get rid of all that worry in my parents' eyes, then everything would be like it was before I got sick. My father would spend time with me again instead of working non-stop. My mother would go back to work instead of staying at home and fussing over me all day. They'd let me go to school and get a pet, and I might even have friends again like I used to. I'm not a wizard, though, and I don't have a magic wand I can wave to make my wishes come true. I fold up the list again—it just makes me feel worse looking at it.

I haven't got "convince my mother to let me go to swimming lessons again" or "become an Olympic champion" on the list, even though that's what I want more than anything. I'll be twelve in a few months, and I know the difference between hoping for the best, and dreaming of the impossible.

I just manage to get the paper hidden away and the bedpost screwed back on before I'm interrupted yet again.

"Adam?" My mother walks straight into my room without knocking. I grit my teeth. It's like being back in the hospital ward where everyone could see me all of the time and there was no escape from the eyes that were always watching me.

"You didn't finish your cake, so I've brought it up with some biscuits and hot chocolate. Would you like me to make you some custard to go with it? Or some ice cream?"

I don't want you to keep bringing me food and making me fat! I want to scream. *I just want you to leave me alone!*

But I don't say that. I just smile weakly and say, "Thanks, Mum."

Mum smiles back. Her eyes are calm again and the panic is gone for now. It's almost worth being locked up in here with no freedom to see that.

Almost…

Chapter 5

NORAH

"Did I show you my perfume, Jenna? It's Chanel. Mum sent it from New York."

Chelsea Mackay pulls out the bottle again and dabs a tiny bit on Jenna's wrist, and Jenna looks like her eyes are going to pop out of her head with excitement. I can smell it from halfway across the playground where I'm leaning against the gate, waiting for Dad to meet me after school. The bell rang fifteen minutes ago, and all the younger kids have already gone home with their parents. Now there's only a few of us hanging round the gates waiting to be picked up. I hate it when Dad's late. When there's no adults watching, the other kids can be as mean as they like to me.

I hunch up as small as I can when Chelsea and her gang of admirers walk past. Most of the kids like me who have to do maths and reading in the special class are treated like dirt by the mainstreamers, but not Chelsea. Even though she lives in a foster home, Chelsea's special. I don't know exactly what it is her mum does in New York, but she must work twenty-four hours a day at something really important, cos otherwise it doesn't make sense that Chelsea has to live here in Hull instead of in New York with her, does it? She makes up for it by sending Chelsea really expensive gifts all the time, and that's why Chelsea's so popular even though she's in my special class and can't count to twenty without using her fingers either.

"Mum says I can stay with her in New York this summer," Chelsea grins. She's got red cheeks and frizzy brown hair, and when she gives a big gap-toothed smile she looks a bit like an apple that someone's taken a bite out of. "She's going to take me round all the big stores to buy stuff, and then we're going to drive around Manhattan in her Ferrari and see the Empire State Building and eat at Planet Hollywood."

The perfume smells like flowers and posh hotels and exotic holidays. Most of all it smells like money. I can't help leaning forward to catch another breath of it as Chelsea passes.

"What are you looking at, you smelly tramp?"

Chelsea catches sight of me, and I can't back off fast enough to hide now.

"Nothing," I mutter. It's not a good idea to speak to Chelsea or her friends. They'll just use anything I say to make fun of me.

"Just as well you've got that perfume, Chelsea, so we can't smell Norah's stinky clothes." Jenna shoots me a mean look and holds her nose.

Chelsea laughs like it's the funniest thing she's ever heard. She knocks into me hard as she passes, and I have to grab the gate so I don't fall down. The rusty hinges scrape my hand, but I pretend it doesn't bother me. They'd only laugh harder if they saw I was hurt. Chelsea turns to smirk back at me as she gets into the car that's waiting for her across the road, and the other girls head down the street in a group, chattering away and exchanging pictures on their phones. They've already forgotten I even exist.

"Are those kids bothering you, pet?" Dad comes hurrying up, out of breath from walking all the way from the job centre on the other side of Hull. He spends most of the week there or in the library, asking the staff to help him apply for jobs that he's never going to get as there's so many people who can actually read properly applying for each one. It's a pointless waste of time, but he has to do it or his benefits money will be cut. I know how useless it makes him feel, and I don't want to make him feel any worse.

"Nah, they're just friends from school," I say. I'm almost as good at lying as Dad is now. I've had lots of practise. He can tell I'm not being honest, I can read it in his eyes, but he lets it go. He's having another rubbish day, and I don't think he can deal with any more bad news right now. His hands are in his pockets again, and his shoulders are even more hunched than usual. I know what that means. He's had to go and ask the council for a foodbank voucher, and he hates doing that more than anything. The local foodbank is at the church we go to, and Dad doesn't like everyone there knowing how poor we are.

It's either that or starve for three whole days, though, cos we've eaten all the spaghetti hoops and instant noodles and there's nothing left in the cupboard. It's only Tuesday, and there won't be any benefits money to buy food until Friday. It's not so bad for me as I get free school lunches, and I can just about manage on that and the mini box of cereal and carton of milk we get each at the B&B. We're supposed to get breakfast included in price of the room, and I thought that meant we'd get bacon and eggs and beans every morning, but a little cereal box that's only big enough for a Barbie doll and a splash of milk is all they ever give us.

When we get to Riverbank Hall we wait around in the queue for a bit before Dad can hand his voucher over and we can get our bags of food. I recognise some of the people in the queue, and I know most of the helpers here from church, but Dad doesn't talk to anyone. He just keeps his head down till it's our turn, like he's really embarrassed. He doesn't take any tea or the biscuits they offer us either, even though he had three cups last Sunday and more biscuits than I could count. Somehow it's different for him coming here to ask for free food when it's not the coffee club that everyone in church goes to. I don't really understand why—it's the same church hall, the same tea and biscuits, and the same cups and plates they use and everything. But it's not a coffee club today, it's a foodbank, and somehow that changes things for him. He lets me have orange juice and as many biscuits as I like while we're waiting, though, so that makes me feel a bit better, even though I'm still confused.

They give us three big carrier bags of food that Dad lifts straight away, shaking his head when one of the Sunday school teachers asks if he'd like some help with them. He just wants to get out as fast as he can. I scurry after him, and he stops as soon as he gets to the end of the car park, out of breath already.

"Give me a bag, Dad, I can carry one," I offer. We don't have the money for the bus fare, and it's a long way back to the B&B.

"It's fine, pet, they're too heavy for you. Give me your school bag, and I'll put some tins in it."

"Only if you let me carry it."

Dad's not happy about that, but he can't take it all by himself. He only puts a few tins and some of the lighter packets like tea and biscuits in my backpack, though, so he's still carrying all the heavy stuff. We set off again, but it's slow going and we have to keep stopping at the end of every road to take a rest. The carrier bags are just ordinary ones like you get from the supermarket – they don't say "foodbank" or "charity" or anything like that. But carrying those bags all the way across town is making Dad's cheeks go red, and not just from effort. I start to wonder if I should be ashamed too, and then I think of what Chelsea Mackay and her mean friends would say if they knew we didn't even have enough money to buy food till Friday and we were getting handouts from the church.

The thought of any of them seeing me makes me hunch my shoulders over too and stare at the ground so hard that soon my whole back is hurting under the weight of my schoolbag.

"You're not happy, pet, are you?" Dad asks, his eyes all sad.

I'm not happy because Dad's not happy. If he didn't mind about not having a job and living in the B&B and having to go to the foodbank, then I wouldn't mind either. I wouldn't even mind so much about being bullied by Chelsea and the other kids and about the rich boy taking my baby birds if I could only see Dad smile for real. I don't know how to say all that without making him feel guilty, so I just shrug and say, "I'm fine."

Dad's frown gets deeper, and he puts his bags down at the bus stop and we sit on the bench to rest for a bit. His hands are red raw from carrying the heavy bags, and my shoulders hurt from all the tins in my backpack, but I pretend I don't notice. Dad's fishing around in his pockets, and he pulls out some coins and counts them. They're the last of the money we've got until Friday. It's not even enough for the bus fare back to the B&B from here, even though we've already walked halfway. His eyes light up when he realises he's missed a pound coin from the last time he counted, and he grins at me. "Hey! There's enough here to get you a sausage roll and maybe even a little cake. Wait here, pet. I'll fetch you something hot for your dinner."

"But we've got our dinner right here." I point to the heavy bags. "There's enough to do us for days and days."

"I know, pet, but it's not hot food is it? I don't want you having cold sandwiches for your dinner."

"There's bread for toast in here, and instant noodles. That'd be hot." I try to sound cheerful, but the smell of sausage rolls and pies and iced buns is wafting across the street and my stomach is gurgling like the washing machines in the laundrette. I can't stand the thought of me scoffing hot bakery food while Dad goes hungry yet again, though. I know he'd just tell me he already ate and wouldn't let me share anything with him.

"I'll be back in a minute." Dad stands up, but I hold onto his jacket.

"I've got a better idea," I say quickly. "Why don't we both have a little treat? We've got enough food to do us, and the money's coming in on Friday, so there's no harm in a bit of fun, is there?"

Dad knows what I'm asking. He hesitates for a minute, then he goes into the newsagents instead of the bakery. Back when we were renting a proper house, we'd always have the same mid-week treat. Dad would get a takeaway—kebabs or a Chinese—and he'd bring home a pile of scratch cards for us to play. Often we wouldn't win anything, but it was lots of fun trying, and the excitement when we did win twenty pounds or even just five pounds was worth weeks of not winning anything. Once we even won a hundred and fifty pounds. Dad got me a trampoline for the back yard with that money. That was the best summer I ever had, and lots of girls from my old school came round to play on it. That was before Dad lost his job and we had to sell everything and move out and everything changed. Things might be different now, but I want that old life back so bad I can taste it. It tastes like sausage rolls and iced buns and warm clean clothes that haven't been bought in charity shops, but maybe I'm remembering it wrong. Maybe it's just the smell from the bakery that's mixing everything up.

While I'm waiting for Dad, a bus pulls up and people get on and off. They all ignore me like I'm not even here, even though our foodbank bags are taking up half the bus shelter. There's a big advert on the side of the bus, and I squint at the words until I can finally read them, mouthing the letters as I go along. "Stand Up and Stand Out," the advert says. There's four teenagers all pouting out at the camera, but one of them's got half her head cut off by a window, so I can't tell if she's as scary-beautiful as the rest. Huh. It's alright for them with their expensive clothes and legs as long as a double-decker bus. If I looked like that and had clothes that cost that much instead of second-hand ones, I wouldn't be scared to stand out in school either. I'd probably be leader of Chelsea's gang, and I'd get picked first in P.E. instead of last. It's easy to stand up for yourself when you've got money to buy as many friends as you want.

Dad comes back out and sits on the bench as the bus pulls away. He's looking nervous, like he thinks he's made a mistake. He only had enough for three scratch cards, and I can tell he thinks he should've bought me a sausage roll with the money after all.

"It's just a bit of fun, remember?" I say quickly, so he knows I'm not regretting the sausage roll too. Dad nods and hands me two cards and a penny to scratch the silver foil off. I want us to take our time, to stretch it out like we used to and do the boxes one by one, pretending we're on some big game show. But the wind is cold and Dad's fingers are sore from carrying the bags, so even though there's still over an hour before we can go back to the B&B, he's rushing and scratching all the silver away in one go. His card's a dud, and he scrunches it up in disgust.

I finish my own card quicker than I'd like, nervous now cos Dad's watching me, willing me to win. I can hear him tutting when none of the fruit pictures match and I'm left holding a useless card. I don't look up, though. I just scratch away at the second card like my life depends on it. This isn't fun like it used to be. I wish I'd never suggested it, and just taken the stupid sausage roll instead. It wouldn't have made me feel sick like this.

Dad suddenly draws in a breath and takes the card off me. I can't see cos there's tears in my eyes and I think he's going to scrunch it up and throw it away too. But then I rub my eyes and I see that he's smiling, and I know right then that everything's going to be OK.

"You did it, Sunny!" he grins. "Fifteen pounds! We're rich!"

Dad's happy, and it makes my heart nearly burst out of my chest to see it. He rushes back to the shop to get the money, then he grabs the bags and leads me across the street to the bakery.

He sits me down at one of the little tables and asks me what I'd like. I can have anything I want—sausage rolls or steak slices or scotch pies—but I don't care which. The whole world smells like delicious hot food and I just know anything I eat now is going to taste like magic.

Maybe our luck is finally changing for the better, I think as Dad waits in the queue to get our food. *Maybe I don't need legs as long as a double-decker bus and expensive clothes to feel ten-feet tall after all.*

If anyone from school saw me having dinner in the bakery, they wouldn't know I was poor and went to a foodbank. I wouldn't mind standing out right now like the advert said if Chelsea Mackay walked past the window. Standing up for myself at school is a bit harder, though. I don't think I'd have the guts to do that no matter how many sausage rolls I won on a scratch card. But there is one other way I can stand up for myself and stop the rich folk with their fancy clothes and long legs looking down on me, and that's to get my baby birds back. That posh prince better look out, cos now that my luck has changed, come Saturday I'm going to march right up to his fairytale castle and steal my nest of birds out from under his turned-up nose.

Chapter 6

ADAM

I thought Saturday was never going to come. My mother cleans and bakes every weekend, so I can spend the day in the garden without being watched. It's been so hard sneaking food to the baby birds every day. You'd think my treehouse was on the other side of the Earth instead of the other side of the garden the way my mother fusses every time I go out the back door. Now I've got a whole afternoon to spend with them, and maybe now that they're ready to fly I can figure out a way to let them go without the neighbour's cat getting them.

I'm just climbing the ladder when I hear something odd. Up in the treehouse, there's the sound of feet crossing floorboards. And I don't mean tiny birds' feet either, I mean real live human feet. I freeze halfway up the steps, wondering if my mother's come to find out why I'm spending so much time out here. If she knew I'd been looking after the baby birds and catching all their germs, she'd be so upset I don't think I could handle it. But I just saw her pulling the storage boxes out from under the stairs to sort through all our old junk for the billionth time. It's her favourite hobby, and she'll be at it for hours. Whoever's up there, it isn't my mother.

It's not my father either. He's in the study making phone calls to his clients. He'll be in there all day. The last place he'd be is in my treehouse, even if I wanted him there. That means there's a stranger in my treehouse, and nobody knows they're up there except me. I hesitate for a bit longer, then I start climbing again.

It can't be a burglar, I think. *They'd steal my father's BMW from the front drive or break into the living room while we were asleep to take our TV and laptops. They wouldn't sneak into a kid's treehouse, would they?*

My head's spinning trying to work it out, and my heart's pounding so hard it's making me dizzy. I haven't felt this alive in years. It's weird—I'm so scared my hands are shaking as I grip the ladder, but I'm so excited at the same time I can't stop myself from clambering up to the platform and pushing open the treehouse door.

"Who's in there?" I demand. Only it doesn't come out like that. It sounds more like a frightened squeak. There's another noise from inside. This one sounds like a cross between a gasp of surprise and a whimper. It makes me feel brave, and I put my head round the door, ready to run back to the safety of my house if I have to.

I don't have to. There's no one in here except a girl with tangled black hair and a guilty look on her face. "You!" I gasp, recognising her as the one I saw riding across the park last week. "What are *you* doing in here?"

She glances down nervously, and that's when I see she's got my nest full of baby birds in her arms and is trying to stuff it into a grubby schoolbag. The birds don't like that. They all jump out of the nest, squawking and flapping round the treehouse trying to fly away. I slam the door shut to stop them escaping and falling out of the tree, and that makes the girl back up against the wall and look at me like I'm an axe murderer. I feel really bad for scaring her, even though she's the one who's trespassing.

"I'm Adam," I say, trying to make it sound friendly this time. "What's your name?"

She whispers something, and I have to ask her twice before I catch it.

"Norah," she says, clutching her empty bag to her chest like I'm going to steal it off her even though there aren't any birds in it anymore.

"What are you doing up here, Norah?" I ask. "You're not supposed to be in other people's gardens without permission. Do your parents know you're here?" She doesn't look old enough to be wandering around on her own.

"I'm not a baby," Norah mutters. "I'm eleven."

"Oh. Me too." We stare at each other for a minute, and I can tell she's thinking the opposite—that I'm too big to be eleven. She says something else that I don't catch, then she takes a deep breath and says it louder, so I'll hear.

"You took my birds. They're mine. I found them and fed them, and then you took them away." She looks like she's going to cry. I hate it when people cry. It always seems to be my fault. The big shiny tears in the corners of her eyes remind me of all the times my mother cried when I was in hospital, and all the times I pretended to be asleep while my father sat by my bedside and nearly choked trying to swallow his sobs. The hurt in Norah's eyes makes me feel terrible. Why do I always have to go and ruin everything for everyone?

"I'm sorry, I didn't know you were feeding them," I say quickly. "Their parents were killed by the cat from next door. If I hadn't brought them up here, she would've killed them too."

"Oh," the girl says. She bites her lip and looks at the birds all flapping happily round the floor, and doesn't seem to know what else to say. She still looks guilty at being caught up here, but at least she doesn't look scared anymore.

"I wanted to release them today," I tell her, trying to coax a smile from her, "but I'm not allowed out of the back garden. If I let them go here, the cat will just get them. Have you got any ideas where to take them?"

All at once, the girl's eyes light up. The tears vanish and she's no longer looking at me like I'm a monster. Her grin's so wide it warms me up like a giant cup of hot chocolate and whipped cream, and I can't help smiling back.

"I know the best place ever!" she says eagerly. "You know the nature trail on the other side of the park?"

"I can see it from here, but..." My face falls. Norah doesn't notice as she's bending down, letting the little birds hop over her hands.

"Well, it's got a big fence to keep dogs and cats out, and it's full of trees and squirrels and places for the birds to hide. I'm going there now to let a mouse I rescued go. Come on, let's go and set the birds free there too." She looks up and sees the big frown on my face, and that makes her look worried again.

"I really want to, Norah, it's just…"

"What? You don't want me to come?" The corners of her mouth tremble. I get the feeling she's been told lots of times by other kids that they don't want her around.

"It's not you, it's my parents," I admit, feeling like a bit of an idiot. "They don't let me leave the garden."

"Why?" It's a simple question, but I don't know how to answer it.

"Umm…" is all I manage to say.

"Are you a vampire who can't go out in the sun? An alien from the planet Zog they're hiding from the government?" She's grinning now, but I don't think she's making fun of me. "Come on, it'll just take fifteen minutes."

I frown again and think hard. It won't take fifteen minutes to get to the nature trail and back. It'll take half an hour at least, probably longer. But if I stay cooped up in this prison for even five more minutes I'll go crazy. I need to get out, and this is the perfect opportunity. If I don't seize it now, then I'll never have the courage to leave by myself.

"OK," I nod, trying to sound brave. "Can you catch that bird there? We'll need to put them all in your bag." I pick one of the fledglings up carefully and put it into Norah's backpack before it can flap away. She manages to gather up a couple more despite them not being too keen on the idea, and we put their nest in too and close the zip, leaving a little space for air. Norah doesn't want to let go of her bag, so I help her loop it back over her shoulders, then I go to the top of the ladder and check that my mother isn't looking out of the kitchen window.

"All clear," I tell her. "We need to be quick so you're not seen."

Norah shoots me a questioning look, but she takes hold of the ladder and does her best to get down as fast as she can. She's a bit clumsy, and she nearly falls off when her foot doesn't connect with one of the rungs. I swallow the warning I nearly cry out and grab her arm instead, helping her down the final steps. With one last look at the house to check for watching eyes, I hurry her to the gate and lift the latch.

I left it unlocked after I rescued the birds last week, just in case.

"Oh! The gate wasn't locked." Norah rolls her eyes. "*Now* you tell me."

I look down and see a rip in the knee of her jeans and a couple of nasty scrapes on her arm from when she must've climbed the fence. I'm impressed. The fence is high, and her coordination isn't too good. She must've been pretty determined to get those birds back to risk a fall like that.

We clamber through the thick trees on the other side of the gate, and then we're out on the path that circles the park. I've never been further than this without my parents. My mother would be out of her mind with worry if she knew I was about to cross the park on my own, stepping into a world full of germs and strangers and unknown dangers she can't hide me from. I can feel the hair on the back of my neck prickling, like I'm standing on the top of a cliff about to jump off with nothing but a bungee rope to break my fall. I saw that once on a travel programme on TV. It looked terrifying, but exciting at the same time. That's exactly how I feel right now.

Norah pulls her bike out from behind a bush and I have to bite back a laugh when I see it despite how nervous I am, because the bike I'd pictured as a wild mustang racing across the prairies still has stabilisers on it. Norah opens the little box attached to the back and carefully puts her bag full of birds next to a hamster cage that has a small brown mouse in it. Then she gets on and starts cycling away down the path without looking back to check if I'm following. She doesn't get how scary this is for me, and I don't want to tell her in case she thinks I'm a total wimp. I hurry to catch up.

My legs are long enough for me to keep up with her bike without jogging, which is just as well, as I'm not fit like I used to be when I was a champion swimmer. Norah's much happier now that we're out of my garden, and she's chattering away so fast it's hard to follow everything she says.

"Do you like animals? I do," she says without waiting for an answer. "I used to have a hamster, but it died, and if I could have anything I'd have a dog, or maybe even two dogs and a cat. Do you have any pets? If I had a really big house out in the country, I'd maybe even have a horse, but it might have to be a Shetland pony otherwise it'd probably be too big for me. There's a really good book about horses in the library. Do you go to the library? I like it in there. I'm not so good at reading, but they've got a whole shelf full of animal books with photos, and the nice lady at the checkout desk sometimes helps me read the instructions about how to look after them."

Norah finally pauses for a breath, and I try to decide which question to answer first. I pick the easiest one, the one where I won't have to explain all about my cancer and my parents and the weird life I'm living right now. "Yeah, I like animals," I say. "I read lots of books about them too. I want to be a vet when I leave school."

That was a good answer, even if it was a lie. Not only does it make Norah smile, but it makes it sound like I actually go to the library and to school like normal people.

"A vet? Wow! That's a great idea. Maybe I can be a vet when I leave school too?"

I smile back, but I don't tell her that you need to study hard and take loads of exams to be a vet, and someone who can't read even though she's nearly finished primary school probably wouldn't pass. I don't tell her that what I really want to be is a champion swimmer, not a vet. I don't want to answer any questions about why I don't swim anymore.

We've skirted the duck pond, and we're passing the playground. I don't think I know any of the parents who are gathered round the swings and slides, but I pull my jacket hood up just in case any of our neighbours are there who might recognise me. "I think it's going to rain," I say to Norah. She looks up at the clear sky, and back at me like I'm off my head. I pick up the pace, hurrying now to reach the far side of the park. Norah pedals faster, her feet fumbling as she tries to keep up. I'm losing my nerve now that I'm so far from the garden, and I just want to get this over with and get back home as fast as I can.

"Wait up!" she calls when I reach the trail gate that keeps dog walkers out. "I've got the birds, remember?"

She gets off her bike and pushes it through the gate I hold open for her. There's a path leading through thick trees, and after only a few steps it feels like we're walking through a forest in a faraway country. Norah's right, this is the perfect place to release the birds. We keep going till we find a good spot where there's some hollow logs and a few shorter trees for the robins to practise flapping up to the branches. Norah lets the mouse go first, waving to it sadly as it scurries round in circles then disappears into the undergrowth. I can tell she doesn't really want to let the birds go, as she hesitates a bit when she opens her backpack, but before she can change her mind the birds all come hopping out and go fluttering about trying to figure out where they are.

"We should've brought some food for them," Norah frowns. "They'll be hungry if they haven't figured out how to find worms for themselves."

"They'll work it out pretty quick—it's crawling with beetles in here. You can give them this for now." I pass her the little bag of berries and grated cheese I put in my pocket before I climbed up to the treehouse.

Norah looks at me in surprise. "Aren't you staying to feed them with me?"

"Can't. Got to get back." My feet are itching to run back across the park before my parents find I'm gone, but I can't help asking, "Don't your parents mind that you're here all by yourself?"

Norah shrugs and turns her attention back to the birds, and I feel a hot spark of envy flash through me. It must be amazing to have parents who let you do whatever you want. If I could swap places with Norah right now, I'd do it in a heartbeat. Just as I'm turning to go, she looks back at me and asks, "Are you coming out again?"

I hesitate. "You mean to the park?"

Norah nods. "Now it's the Easter holidays, I'll probably be here most days. We can check on these birds and see if there are any more animals that need rescued. It'll be fun." She's trying to smile, but there's a pleading look on her face that says she'll be hurt if I say no.

I think hard for a second, hearing my mother's disapproving voice in my head and seeing the worry in her eyes. My common sense is telling me that meeting Norah in secret ever again is probably a really, really bad idea. For once, I decide not to listen.

"Maybe on Monday," I say quickly before I can change my mind. "Come to the back gate at about two o'clock, but don't knock. Wait for a bit—if I can come out I will, but if not, you'll have to go on without me."

Norah nods, just about satisfied with that, and I turn and run all the way back across the park with a bubble of fear and excitement filling my chest so full I can barely breathe.

Chapter 7

NORAH

I haven't been this happy in a long time. Ever since we won money on that scratch card my luck's been brilliant. Dad's stayed away from Ed and the betting shop, and he's gone to fill in all his job applications like he's supposed to. Chelsea and her gang were too busy talking about the coming holidays to pay any attention to me at school yesterday, and best of all that posh prince turned out to be a nice boy today, even if he does wear the same expensive clothes as those models on the side of the bus.

Adam's a bit odd, but I think I like him. He didn't get mad when I sneaked into his treehouse, and he was good about letting me set the birds free with him. I think he's just pretending his parents are really strict, though, cos he doesn't want to hurt my feelings. I know he doesn't want to admit they'd be angry if they knew he was hanging out with a homeless person like me. They probably wouldn't want me near the house in case I'd steal all their fancy stuff just because I'm poor.

I didn't tell Adam about Dad losing his job and our house, but I think he could probably guess from my clothes and the fact I've got to hang about the park on my own all Saturday while Dad goes to the job centre. I don't think Adam cares about that, though. I think I might have a friend at last, and that makes me smile. Now all I need is a real pet and I'll be halfway to crossing off all the things on my special list.

I'm cycling past the boarded-up bingo hall when I see him—number three on my list. He's sitting in the alley shivering, his hair more tangled than mine. Dad runs a brush through my curls every morning and he even used to do plaits for me, but my hair's got a mind of its own and they always came undone by lunchtime. I've lost a small fortune in bobbles and scrunchies over the years, and Dad's given up buying packs of new ones now that every fifty pence has to count for something. This dog doesn't have anyone to brush his hair, though. He's so skinny I don't think he's got anyone to feed him either.

I stop pedalling and pull the brakes. The dog shuffles round the back of the bins to hide, but even though he's whimpering, his tail's wagging so hard against them it sounds like he's playing the drums. He pokes his head back out, and we sit looking at each other for a bit. He makes the first move, shuffling forward on his belly till he's just about in reach. I don't stretch my hand out, cos I know that would just scare him off. Instead, I get off my bike and open the cargo box at the back where I've got my empty hamster cage. That's not what I'm looking for, obviously. You can't fit a dog in there, even if he is just a little Highland terrier.

"Is this what you're looking for?" I ask, holding out the other half of the corned beef sandwich Dad made me for lunch with the last of the foodbank donation. I was saving it for dinner in case there's a problem with the benefits money again, but this dog looks like he needs it more than me. He whines and shuffles even closer. He's desperate for the food, but he's afraid to take it out of my hand. I put it on the ground for him and step back so he knows I'm not going to hurt him. He goes for the sandwich straight away, gobbling it up so fast it's gone in one swallow. Then he edges right up to me and paws my jeans, asking for more. I bend down and pat him gently, even though his hair's so grubby he looks like he's grey instead of white.

"Sorry, boy, that's all I've got. Maybe you can have some more if you come with me?" I get back on the bike and pedal away, and when I look back, the dog's following behind me with his tail wagging. I want to take my list out and cross off number three right there and then, but Dad's waiting for me and he'll be worried if I'm late.

The library's not far from the park, otherwise Dad wouldn't let me go there on a Saturday instead of staying with him all day while he fills out his forms. He's supposed to prove he spends twenty-five hours a week applying for jobs, but if you count all the time walking into town and waiting in line at the library or job centre, it's pretty much a full-time job just proving he's *looking* for a full-time job. We don't have a computer and he needs help to fill in the forms, so the only time he can do it is if someone at the job centre or the library helps him. There's never enough staff, so that means he usually doesn't fill in enough forms, and the benefits people keep taking money off him. It's not fair. Dad doesn't want to be on benefits, but there's just not enough jobs out there for everyone who wants one.

I chain my bike up outside the library with the little padlock that came with it, and tell the dog to stay. Whoever owned him before didn't train him very well, cos he doesn't listen, he just follows me. Luckily the door's a revolving one and he's scared of it, so I manage to get in without him. I need a minute to explain things to Dad before I try to persuade him to adopt something that looks and smells like it's been used to mop the floors of a stink-bomb factory. I really, *really* hope he's having a good day.

Dad's not at the computers where I'm expecting to find him, though. When I have a look round, I see him standing near the coffee counter in the cafe section. I'm about to go over, but just then I see he's not on his own. There's a woman standing with him, and it looks like they're having a big argument. The woman's got dark curly hair, and I think she'd probably be pretty if she wasn't scowling so hard. She's poking a finger in Dad's chest like she's accusing him of something, and he's frowning and snapping right back. Finally the woman pulls a card of her handbag and hands it to him, and Dad rips it in two and yells, "You can't have her, she's mine!" so loud that other people in the library turn to stare.

The woman shakes her head and storms off, and I hope my new dog has enough sense to stand well back from the revolving door when she comes out or he's going to end up spinning round and round like he's in a washing machine. I hurry over to Dad. When he sees me, he stuffs the ripped pieces of card into his pocket so I don't see them. "Hi, pet," he says, trying to paste a smile on his face. "How was the park?"

He's not getting out of it that easily. "Who was that woman?" I ask straight away.

"Who?" Dad's trying to look innocent, but it's not working.

"*Her*," I say, pointing to the door. Oh. She's gone.

"Umm, just someone who thought I skipped the queue for the computer, that's all," Dad shrugs. "Don't worry about it. Look, Norah, I've got a bit of bad news." Dad hesitates, and I can see little worry lines forming at the corners of his eyes. This is going to be bad. *Really* bad.

"They got the benefits wrong again, pet," he sighs. "They've hardly put any money in my account. When I phoned they said I didn't apply for enough jobs and I missed two appointments with a work coach, but they haven't replaced the two faulty computers at the job centre, and the work coach called in sick both times I was meant to meet him, so what was I supposed to do?"

I know it's not Dad's fault he's lost out on most of the money this month, but it's a big problem, and not just because it means we'll be struggling for food. "What about the rent at the B&B?" I ask. "Mrs Crabbit said we couldn't stay any longer if we didn't pay today." My voice has gone all wobbly as there's a big lump in my throat. I know this is bad, cos I can see all the lines on his face getting deeper.

"Let me worry about that, pet. We'll go back just now and I'll talk some sense into her, OK?"

"OK, Dad." I swallow the lump and try to give a cheerful wave to the woman who works at the checkout desk as we pass, cos I don't want the whole world knowing we're in trouble yet again. I don't want folk thinking it's Dad's fault and he isn't looking after me properly just because the stupid job centre is always making a mess of things for us.

The bad news is so bad that I've totally forgotten about the dog.

As soon as I get outside he goes nuts, jumping all over me and wagging his tail like I've come back from the dead instead of just the library. Dad takes one look at him, and I can tell right there and then that whatever I ask him for, the answer's going to be no.

"For goodness' sake, Norah," he mutters, "can't you stop picking up stray animals for five minutes? I'm not running a bloody zoo."

I don't ask him if I can keep the dog. He's too stressed about the rent, and when he's got a lot on his mind sometimes mean things slip out of his mouth before he can stop them. I don't want those mean things to be about me, so I unlock my bike without patting the dog so he knows I'm not going to play anymore. "Sorry, boy," I say sadly, "you'll have to go somewhere else."

Dad walks so fast I have to pedal as hard as I can. When I look back the dog's still following me, but I can see he's getting tired. His little legs just can't keep up. I look away before it makes me cry. We're in trouble and Dad needs me to be strong right now, and that means no begging him for pets that I know I can't have, and no getting upset about things that can't be helped.

We head across the city centre and then cut through one of the estates to get to the B&B. My legs are getting sore and the bike is starting to feel heavy, and I feel bad when we have to stop a couple of time so I can catch my breath. We have to get back quickly so we can explain to the manager why we're not paying the rent again even though we're supposed to pay for it out of Dad's benefits. I know Dad wants me to forget all about the dog, but when we cross the road, I can't help looking back. He's not following me anymore. He's sitting in the cargo box that I forgot to shut, squashed up against the hamster cage and hitching a ride back with me.

I bite back the grin that's threatening to split my face in half and cycle the rest of the way with my big secret in tow. It doesn't stay secret for long. Dad swears at the dog when we get to the B&B and throws a stick at him to make him run back down the street yelping. I don't have time to say anything about that, though, as he tells me to go straight upstairs while he sorts things out with the Crabbits. He just leaves my bike in the yard, so I know he doesn't think we're going to be allowed to stay. That makes me feel even worse than him scaring the dog.

I walk round and round our room till I'm dizzy, then I stop and sit for a bit on the windowsill watching Boris eat a fly. I can't see the dog outside cos our room looks out onto the back of the house, but I can see further down the estate to the other houses where people with jobs live. There's a trampoline in one of the gardens, just like the one I used to have. Before I can help myself, I'm dreaming that things will turn out OK. Maybe the Crabbits will let us live here for a bit longer until Dad finds a job and we have enough money to rent a real house, and I'll be able to keep the dog and even have a trampoline like I used to. Maybe—

Dad comes back in and slams the door. One look at his face tells me things aren't going to be OK. "What did they say?" I ask, afraid to hear the answer.

"We have to leave. They say I've been promising them rent since we moved in, and since it's not been paid, we have to move out today. Pack your stuff—we need to find somewhere else."

Dad starts opening drawers and throwing clothes into his big suitcase, but I just stand there stunned. "We haven't paid *any* rent?" is all I can say. "But we've been here nine weeks!"

I might not be any good at counting, but I've been ticking the days off in my school notepad. The council isn't supposed to let families stay in B&Bs for more than six weeks without moving them somewhere better, but after our last hostel closed down, they didn't have anywhere else to put us.

"We've not had the money, alright?" Dad snaps, sounding mean. "They've got another family waiting downstairs for the room, so we need to leave. Start putting your things away, OK? I need to phone the housing office before they close for the day."

I just nod without saying anything else, scooping Boris up into an empty matchbox that I hide in the pocket of my jeans.

Dad's scared, and it's making me scared too. If we don't find somewhere to stay tonight and social services finds out about it, then I could get taken away from Dad and put in a foster home like Chelsea Mackay. She pretends she likes it there, but I know she'd give anything to go and live in New York with her mum instead. The thought of being split up from Dad and made to live with strangers makes me cry, and I can hardly see through my tears to pack my bags. We've moved so many times we've not got much stuff anymore, so it doesn't take us too long.

Dad manages to get all of our bags downstairs in two trips, and as he's hauling the big suitcase out the door, we pass the other family who's getting our room. There's two kids who are younger than me, and a baby too, so it's going to be a tight fit. I should probably warn them about the broken lamp by the bed and the hot tap in the bathroom that doesn't work, but Dad's hurrying me out into the cold and there's no time. We drag all of our bags to the bus shelter at the end of the road, and Dad calls the housing office. It starts off polite, but by the time he hangs up he's swearing.

"Are they not going to give us another room?" I ask nervously.

Dad shakes his head, looking like he's ready to smash the phone on the ground. "They say paying the rent was my responsibility and that I've made us intentionally homeless by getting kicked out! How can I pay rent if my benefits keep getting cut?"

I don't think he expects an answer to that, so I just swing my legs and stare at my shoes. Dad tries a housing charity next. I really hope they'll give us somewhere for the weekend. The bench is cold and my bum's going numb. Halfway through the phone call, Dad walks a bit further down the road so I can't hear what he's saying. I catch something about social services, so I think that's who they're telling him to call. There's no way Dad's doing that.

I swing my legs harder to warm them up, and my feet nearly connect with a hairy little head that's got a pink tongue sticking out of its mouth. The dog's back, and he's looking just as hungry as me. I bend down and pat him so he knows he's a good dog and none of this is his fault.

Dad's scowling even harder when he walks back, but I don't think it's because of the dog. "Nothing?" I ask. Dad just shakes his head. My stomach's in knots now, and I'm starting to feel sick. This happened once before when they mixed up his benefits. We ended up riding the night bus round Hull two nights in a row till they admitted they'd made a mistake and paid Dad the money. If social services had found out about *that*…

It's getting late, and the wind is cold. I let the little dog snuggle into my jacket and curl up next to me so we can share the warmth. I don't want to spend all night sitting on the bus, but I don't want Dad to call social services and have someone come and take me away either. "Is there anyone else you can call?" I bite my lip, scared the answer will be no.

"There's one other person." Dad walks away again and makes another call. I don't usually pray for things as I'm not sure there's anyone up there listening, but I can't help praying that Dad won't run out of credit before he can make his last call. That's not too much to ask, is it?

When Dad comes back this time, he's not smiling, but he's not scowling anymore either. "Ed says we can stay with his family for a bit till we find somewhere," he says. "The taxi's on its way, so it won't be much longer. Thank goodness for Ed. He's a good mate, eh?"

No, he's not, I think, but I don't say anything as I'm too cold and hungry and anywhere's better than the night bus. Dad nudges the dog away with his foot and sits next to me, rubbing my hands to warm them till the taxi arrives. We manage to get most of our suitcases packed inside with the driver's help, but he's not too happy about squeezing my bike into the back alongside me.

"What about the dog?" I call just before Dad slams the door.

"Don't make a fuss, Norah, not tonight," Dad mutters, shutting me in with a mountain of suitcases and my bike while he goes to sit in the front with a heavy bag on his lap. There's not much wriggle room, but when the taxi drives off I manage to turn and look out of the back window. The dog's running down the road after us, barking like mad. He gets further and further away as we pick up speed until he's only a grubby white dot in the distance. Then we turn onto the main road, and he's gone. I didn't get a chance to say goodbye, not to him, or to Kim and Ollie or to the nice lady on the first floor who sometimes bought me a packet of crisps on her shopping day. They'll only know I'm gone when they knock on my door and find new people in my room.

It's pointless wanting friends or a pet, just like it's pointless Dad trying to get another job when he can't read. I should tear my stupid list up into little bits and scatter the pieces out of the window, but there's so many bags pressing against me I can't reach my pocket. Maybe Dad's right. I'm too old for Santa, and I'm too old to believe that if I just wish hard enough, we can have a nice house with nice things in it like we used to. I need to grow up, and I need to stop believing that dreams can come true.

Chapter 8

ADAM

"Are you going out to the treehouse again?"

I can hardly see my mother past all the vases of flowers and bunches of leaves that are filling the kitchen, but I can hear the surprise in her voice.

"That's where I'm doing my climate change project over Easter," I tell her. "My tutor's given me lots of books to read about it, so I'll be there till dinner time. I'll be back about five o'clock, is that OK?" I hate lying to my mother, but I'm so desperate to get out my fingers are tingling as I reach for the back door handle. I spent ages yesterday carrying books and printouts about global warming up to the treehouse to make it look like I was preparing to spend the Easter holidays studying up there. I don't know if Norah will be waiting for me at the back gate like she said, but if she is, then I want to make sure my mother won't come looking for me till dinner time.

"I suppose so, but if you're cold come straight back in, alright?" She pulls an armful of ferns from a big box and disappears behind a screen of greenery. Her latest hobby to keep her busy around the house while she supervises me is flower arranging for the local church. She hasn't got the hang of it yet, so I should be able to slip away for a few hours unnoticed while she fights with a forest of roses and carnations.

"OK, see you later." I hurry out before she can change her mind. My heart's beating fast as I jog down our long garden, but instead of heading for the treehouse ladder I circle round it and pass through the bushes to the back gate. Before I reach it, there's a sudden knocking sound from the other side. That makes my heart thump so loud I can almost hear it, and I glance back guiltily to make sure my mother's not looking out of the window. Even if she wanted to, she couldn't see out today, though. There are so many vases of flowers piled on the windowsill it's like our kitchen's been turned into the botanical gardens I used to love visiting in London before I got sick.

"Norah!" I hiss, "I told you not to knock!"

"Well, get a move on, then," she whispers from the other side of the fence. "I've been waiting here for hours!"

She doesn't sound annoyed, just excited, like me. She came after all, and I'm so happy I'd be singing if my throat wasn't so tight with nerves. I undo the gate latch and join Norah on the other side of the fence. When we get out onto the path, I can see her smile isn't as bright as it was the last time I saw her.

"Are you alright?" I ask. She looks tired, and there are bags under her eyes.

"Yeah, just didn't get much sleep. I've got sort of…noisy neighbours," she mutters.

"Really? I thought everyone was really quiet here at night." As soon as it's out I bite my tongue. Of course she doesn't live around here. The houses next to the park are full of families with paid cleaners and laundry rooms, and Norah's wearing the same ripped jeans and T-shirt as Saturday, only there's some jam stains on her collar as well now. She shuffles her feet and stares down at her scuffed shoes, then she changes the subject.

"You want to go to the nature trail and see if the baby birds are still there?"

I nod eagerly, holding up a bag of seeds and cake crumbs I've been saving. Her grin's a bit wider this time, and she gets on her little bike and cycles off across the park. It's busier now it's the Easter holidays, but it's mostly parents with younger kids who play on the swings and couples who are sunbathing on the grass. Norah shoots me another one of those funny looks when she sees I've got my jacket hood up again, but I take it off and tie it round my waist when we reach the nature trail, so she doesn't say anything. It's a lot quieter in here, and since it's a Monday any neighbours who might recognise me are probably at work.

We head round to the spot where we left the birds on Saturday, but when we get there, we can't see them in the undergrowth, and the hollow log on the ground is empty too. Norah's face falls, and she slumps down on the log like she's given up hope. "They're gone," she sighs. "Maybe they got eaten by foxes. Maybe bringing them here was a stupid idea."

She looks so sad I don't know what to say. It's like all of the spark has gone out of her since Saturday and she can't imagine anything good happening ever again. But just then I hear a chirping sound in the trees, and I look up and see something brilliant.

"Norah, look!" I point with a big grin on my face. Norah lifts her head and sees one of the little birds balancing on a tree branch. Our baby robins have learned to fly after all. I dig out the bag of seeds I brought and scatter them on the ground, and soon all five fledglings and a couple of bigger blackbirds have fluttered down and are pecking at the food. Norah's trying not to move and scare them away, but she can't help wriggling on the log in excitement.

"We did it, Adam, we saved them!" she says, and her warm smile's back even brighter than before. "We're going to be vets when we leave school for sure!"

I smile back and try to change the subject before she gets her heart set on something she'll probably never get the chance to do. "So... *Norah*," I say, "that's an unusual name. Are you named after your mother?"

Her smile fades a bit and she looks away. "No, I don't have a mother." The way she says it I get the feeling she usually doesn't tell anyone that, so I scoot closer on the log so she can see up close just how sorry I am. "I don't mean she's dead or anything, or she doesn't want to live with me," she says quickly, "so you don't need to feel sorry for me."

"I don't, I just…" I probably shouldn't ask her about it, but I want to get to know her, and I can't work out the puzzle on my own. "So if she's still alive, do you mean you just don't see her?" I try.

Norah rolls her eyes. "No, I mean I never had a mother. Dad says the scientists grew me in a lab in a test tube. It's amazing what they can do these days."

That really doesn't help clear up the confusion. "You can't *not* have a mother," I frown, "Even if you're a test-tube baby, someone still had to give birth to you. That person's your mother. Don't you know who it is?"

The way her eyes go wide I can tell I've said the wrong thing, so I backtrack again. "Anyway, Norah's a nice name. I think I had a great aunt called Norah, but that was a billion years ago and I never met her."

Norah's still biting her lip, but she wants to change the subject too. "I don't know who I'm named after," she shrugs. "I think Dad just liked the name. He calls me 'Sunny' sometimes instead."

"Why?"

"Cos my name's Norah Day—'Sunny Day', get it? And cos he says I'm like my favourite banana-sunshine milkshake. That's when he's having a really good day. When he's having a bad day he says…" Norah closes her mouth suddenly and swallows hard. I try to think of something to change the subject again, but she gets there first. "What does your dad call you?"

"Adam." I shrug. I don't tell her that he really does have a nickname for me. He hasn't used it since I got sick, and remembering that makes me feel terrible.

"Oh. That's a bit rubbish. Not your name," she says quickly, "I mean not having a nickname. I'll have to think of one for you."

I like my own name just fine, but I don't want to tell her that and make her think I'm being unfriendly. I'm not sure if I'm supposed to call her "Sunny" or not, so I just stick to "Norah".

"Are you hungry, Norah?" I ask, pulling out the little picnic I've packed in my bag. I've got some chicken legs I found in the fridge, two cans of Coke and slices of Mum's chocolate cake. Norah's eyes go wide when she sees them and she nods eagerly. We tuck in while we watch the birds eat, but my mother already made me a big lunch and I really want to lose weight, so I let Norah eat most of the picnic. The speed she's eating, I get the feeling she hasn't had much food today.

"This is a good spot you picked," I say while she gobbles up a second piece of cake. "Do you come here a lot with your dad?" I'm trying to find out why she's allowed out so much on her own, but she dodges the question.

"I like coming here to leave flowers for Mrs Nibbles," she says, wiping her mouth on the edge of her T-shirt and leaving a big chocolate stain on it.

"Who?"

"Mrs Nibbles, my pet hamster." She points to a small stone that has a bunch of dried-up wild flowers next to it. "That's where I buried her when she died last month."

"Oh, sorry. But that's so cool you're allowed to have pets. I've been begging my mother and father for a dog for ages. Even a rabbit or a guinea pig would do, but they just say no."

"I'm not allowed pets either," she says, scuffing her feet against the ground and making the birds flutter back in alarm.

"But you had a hamster!"

"Yeah, but that was from before…"

"Before what?"

Norah doesn't answer that, she just asks, "Have you never had a pet, then? Not even a hamster?"

"Years ago," I tell her. "I used to have a dog called Benjy when I was little, but that was before…" I stop dead. I don't want to tell her I was sick and have her look at me the way some of the kids at my old school did when I started going to hospital and lost all my hair. They pretended to be nice about it, but I could see the way they hung back when I tried to talk to them, like they were afraid my cancer was something they could catch.

"Before what?" Norah asks.

I just shrug and look for a way to change the subject yet again. "You want to have a look around to see if there are any animals in here that need rescued?"

Norah grins at that idea. I shove the empty food bags into my backpack and she tucks her bike behind a big tree just in case anyone comes along the path and spots it. Then we head off through the trees to explore the nature trail. There's hardly anyone in here, even though it's the holidays and the swing park's full of kids. The only people we pass on the whole circuit are an old man taking pictures of butterflies in a patch of bluebells and a young woman reading under a tree. I don't think most people know the nature trail is open to the public, and the big gate and "No Dogs" sign puts them off. That suits me just fine. The less people who might recognise me and tell my mother they saw me sitting in the dirt examining beetles, the better.

It's not just beetles we find. It's butterflies and ladybirds and spiders' webs as big as car wheels. We have a competition to see who can spot the most birds' nests in the trees, which I win, and Norah finds a patch of fungus that looks like a fairy village. We're on our hands and knees examining the toadstools, when Norah gasps, "Oh! Look!"

I follow her finger and see that she's pointing at two big stones sitting under a massive oak tree. I don't know why she thinks they're so special, but she's already hurrying over before I can ask. When I follow her, I find it's not the stones she's looking at, but what's fallen in between them. There's a hedgehog squirming around in the narrow space, stuck fast. I know from my animal books that they mostly come out at night, so this one must've been trapped upside down in there for hours.

It looks like it's out of energy and has got really weak trying to free itself.

"We need to get it out!" Norah says, sticking her hand in the crack between the rocks and trying to reach it before I can warn her not to. "Ow!" The frightened hedgehog curls into a tight ball, and Norah gets a fistful of prickles for her trouble.

"We need to find another way to do it," I tell her, looking for a long stick while she sucks her stinging fingers. When I've got one, we take turns putting it down the crack and levering the hedgehog up gently. It's not happy about being disturbed, and flails about like it thinks we're trying to eat it, but eventually we manage to prise it up far enough that it can claw its way out. It sits curled up in a ball on top of the stones for a long time till it finally figures out it's not on the menu, then it dashes off into the undergrowth so fast it nearly trips over its own paws.

"Yes!" Norah cheers. "We're an *awesome* animal rescue team!"

We exchange high fives, and that's when I notice my watch says its already well after four o'clock. It's not dinner time yet, but if I don't head back now, there's a chance my mother will come looking for me in the treehouse, and then I'll be in trouble.

"I've got to go," I say unwillingly, grabbing my backpack before she can talk me into staying any longer. "But maybe we can meet up again tomorrow?"

Norah's face falls. "Oh. I can't get back out again till Thursday."

"But you said you'd be here every day in the Easter holidays!"

"Yeah, but that was before…" There's that word again, the one that neither of us wants to explain. "I've got to do babysitting for the next two days," she finishes in a rush.

"Babysitting? You've got brothers and sisters?"

"No, but…it's complicated. I'll explain next time, OK?"

"OK. See you on Thursday. Two o'clock again? And no knocking on the gate this time!" I want to know more about this girl with the sunshine smile and the flashing silver bike, and I'm willing to wait a few days to find out her secrets as long as it means she'll spend another afternoon with me. She waves as I jog off down the trail, and I keep looking back and waving till she's long out of sight behind the trees.

I'm halfway across the park again before the knot of anxiety tightens in my stomach. I'd almost forgotten it was there, but when I creep back into the garden through the gate, it's so big it's pressing against my chest and I can barely breathe. The back garden's empty, though, and the flower vases are still on the kitchen windowsill.

No, I'm wrong. The back garden's not empty.

The ginger cat is stalking round our fishpond, looking like she's ready to strike. I'm already out of breath from running across the park, but I race over before she can stick her paw in and claw out any of Dad's ornamental goldfish. She hisses at me and backs away, her face all scrunched up and mean, but when she sees I'm not going to budge she slinks away, her tail swishing angrily.

Stupid cat. The world would definitely be a better place if it was a cat-free zone.

I wait for a bit to make sure she doesn't come back, giving myself time to get my breath back so my mother doesn't know I've been running, then I push the back door open. The kitchen's still full of flowers, but at least now they're all arranged in vases, even if some of the roses have been cut too short and the ferns are sticking out at funny angles.

"Oh, Adam, good timing. I was just about to come and get you," my mother says, stirring a saucepan on the cooker. I sneak a look at my watch. Four fifty. That's how long I'll have in future before she comes to the treehouse. Good to know.

"Can you ask your father if he's joining us for dinner? It's a vegetable curry—it'll be ready in twenty minutes."

I drag my feet all the way to the study. I've had such a good day for once. I don't want to end it with disappointment. I knock on the door softly then let myself in. "Dad? Are you having dinner with us? It'll be ready soon."

My father looks up from his computer briefly. His black hair's the same colour as mine, only it's a bit longer since he didn't lose it to cancer, and it's going a bit grey above his ears. He looks tired. "Thanks, son, but I'll get myself something later. I'm in the middle of a pile of reports right now that can't wait."

"Oh." I turn to go, but I don't want my good day to finish this way, the way it always does. "Me and Mum might watch a DVD later on.

Do you want to watch it with us? It's one of those alien invasion ones that you like."

Dad's deep in his computer reports again, and he shakes his head. I'm not even sure he heard me. I'm about to close the door, when Dad looks up suddenly.

"Adam, have you been running round the garden or something?"

My hand freezes on the door handle. "No. Why?"

"Oh. You look like you've been exercising, that's all. It's not a bad look," he says quickly, so I know he's not worried I'm sick or anything. "It suits you. Makes you look…healthy."

Dad smiles, a real smile this time, not the fake one he uses whenever he makes excuses for not playing games with me or eating dinner at the table. I smile back. Dad's noticed me again, and that feels brilliant.

It's not the same as spending time together like we used to, but it's a start.

Chapter 9

NORAH

Living at Ed's flat is like camping out in the middle of a busy funfair in summer. Only it's not fun and there's no sunshine here. What I mean is it's crammed full of people—crying kids and shouting adults—and all the rooms smell of stale smoke and chip grease. I'm supposed to be writing a holiday diary for homework over Easter, but I've been so busy babysitting I haven't written a single word in it yet. The only place I can get peace for five minutes is the bathroom, so I lock myself in there with my schoolbag and spread my jotters and pens over the floor.

I'm rubbish at spelling, and writing anything takes me forever. If I could write long essays in neat handwriting like Chelsea's best friend Jenna, then my holiday diary would go something like this:

Saturday 10th April

First day of the Easter holidays. Got kicked out of our B&B today as Dad's benefits money got mixed up yet again. This happens all the time, and whenever Dad gets a job for a few months it's worse as it takes the benefits people ages to get our money right again once the job's finished. Had to move all our stuff to Ed's flat and leave my new pet dog behind. I've called him "Bingo" cos I found him next to a bingo hall, but I don't think I'll ever see him again, so it's stupid even giving him a name.

Sunday 11th April

Really tired today as I didn't get any sleep. There's only two bedrooms here, and as well as Ed, Cheryl and their five kids, Cheryl's brother's living here too. He says he works in "consumer acquisitions" and I thought that meant a fancy job in the city, but Dad says that just means he nicks stuff and sells it down the local market. Dad and me slept in the living room last night, him on the sofa and me in a sleeping bag, but Cheryl and Ed were arguing till late, then baby Mikie was crying for hours, and everyone kept walking through the living room to get to the toilet and kitchen all night.

Monday 12th April

The best day ever! I went to meet Adam in the park, and we spent all afternoon in the nature trail rescuing animals. I crossed "get a friend" off my wish list, even though I don't know if a posh boy like him really would want to be my friend if I told him the truth about my life and where I live. Had to add a new thing onto the list, though. Number five is "Ask Dad about my mother". Adam says everyone has a mother, and I'm really confused cos I don't know if it's true or not. I'd like to have one, but not if it turns out she abandoned me in the hospital cos she didn't want me. I was itching to ask Dad about that all evening, but didn't get the chance as we couldn't even get five minutes to ourselves.

Dad came back really late with Ed. He said he was at the job centre, but I know he was lying. I think he was at the betting shop again. I'm starting to worry he doesn't really just watch the TV there like he says he sometimes does, and he's gambling our benefits instead. Maybe that's my fault for making him buy those scratch cards and getting him hooked. I'm scared we're going to end up owing money to bad people like Mad Dog Marty back at the B&B who lent cash to some of the families there, then banged on their doors in the middle of the night, shouting that he wanted them to pay back double.

Tuesday 13th April
Worst day ever. Had to babysit Ed's kids while Cheryl took Mikie to the doctor for his cough. Danny's a menace, and I had to keep lifting him off the kitchen counters cos he was climbing up to reach the biscuit cupboard. I thought three-year-old Kayla was a sweetheart till she kicked a tantrum cos I wouldn't let her draw on the walls with her crayons. Chris is nine and should know better than to hit Danny whenever he wants a toy off him, and Toby just follows his big brother around and copies everything he does, so it was like World War Three till Cheryl got back and yelled at them all to stop carrying on. Dad was back late again. I think Ed's turning him into a gambling addict like the ones in the TV shows Cheryl watches. Didn't get a chance to ask Dad if I really do have a mother today either.

Wednesday 14th April
Can you die if you don't get enough sleep? My head feels like it's going to explode. I'm sitting in the loo writing this cos there isn't a quiet space in the whole house. Had to babysit again

as Cheryl went over to a friend's house, but at least she took the baby and Kayla, so it was just Danny and the older boys I had to stop from killing each other till she got back. There's not much to eat in the house cos Ed spends all of his money down at the bookies, and Dad's been buying dinner for everyone with his benefits money. I don't think he's got much left even though he just got paid on Friday. I wish I could count better and add up all our expenses. Then I'd know whether he was telling the truth about not spending money at the betting shop with Ed or not. I don't mind Dad lying to me about small stuff like not being hungry or whether Santa's real, but I'm scared he's lying to me about big stuff too, like why we never have any money and whether I really do have a mother or not.

That's what I'd write if I was good at writing, but I'm not. I grip my pen hard and get as far as *"Satrday 3rid Aeprl"* when Ed's wife Cheryl bangs on the door.

"Norah, love, are you done in there? Danny's peed his pants again and I need to stick a nappy on him."

I sigh and gather up my paper and pens. Danny's four and should know how to use the toilet by now, but with two older brothers, a three-year-old sister and baby Mikie to look after, Cheryl just hasn't had the time to potty-train him properly yet. There's no point trying to write my homework diary now cos the TV in the living room is turned up full blast, Chris and Toby are having a pillow fight in one of the bedrooms, and Cheryl's brother is snoring like a chainsaw in the other. I try to be useful instead, and gather up the clothes that Dad and me need washed as well as any of the kids' stuff I find on the floor.

I'm just carrying the laundry basket through to the kitchen when I hear Dad's voice on the landing behind the front door. He's back early and without Ed, so he must've gone to the job centre or library to fill in job searches like he's supposed to. I heave a big sigh of relief. I'm about to go out and say hello, when I hear what he's saying on the phone.

"How the hell did you get this number?" he demands, sounding really angry. "I told you, I don't want anything to do with you or your parents, not after what you put me through when Norah was born. She's mine. That's the court's decision, and if you contact me again or ambush me in the library like last time, I'll call the police."

He lowers his voice and walks away further down the hall, so I don't catch what he says next, but what I just heard makes all the hair on the back of my neck stick up. When I set the laundry basket down in the kitchen, I realise my hands are shaking. There's something going on, something big that Dad hasn't told me about, and it's about when I was born. That's the second time I've heard Dad tell that mystery woman from the library that I was his. Why would Dad have to tell her that, like she didn't believe him?

A lump of fear begins to grow in my throat. What if I'm adopted, and now my original parents want me back? Or what if…Oh. The next thought has my heart racing so hard I think I'm going to be sick. What if Dad *stole* me from the hospital when I was born, and is just pretending I'm his? What if it's not just Dad skipping meals so I can eat, and telling me he's going to the job centre instead of the betting shop that he's lying about? What if *everything* in my whole life up till now has been a lie?

My brain's whirring round like a broken washing machine, and that reminds me I should put the laundry on before someone comes in here and sees me staring into space with my mouth open. This isn't the kind of house where you can keep secrets, and I don't want to talk about my personal business with a bunch of strangers.

I'm checking the pockets for coins and tissues before I put the clothes in the machine, when I find something in the jeans that Dad was wearing on Saturday. It's the two pieces of the business card the woman gave him in the library. I hold them together and read the small writing on them slowly.

"Sandra Gibson. Rainbow Children's Centre, Grimsby."

There's a couple of phone numbers underneath that, and a little rainbow logo in the corner. I've never heard of the "Rainbow Children's Centre" before, but I bet I can guess what it is. It's probably the kind of home that kids are taken to before they find someone to foster them, like Chelsea Mackay. That woman from the library must be a social worker, and she wants to take me into care because she doesn't think Dad's looking after me right. But what's it got to do with her parents like

Dad said on the phone? What did they put Dad through when I was born, and what did he mean about the "court decision"?

Argh! I'm so confused and scared right now I can't think straight.

"Hi, Norah, what are you up to?"

Dad comes into the kitchen, and I spin round so fast I knock over the laundry basket.

"Nothing. Just putting the washing machine on."

When Dad's setting the basket upright again, I shove the pieces of card into my own pocket, next to my wish list that now has "Ask Dad about my mother" on it. In my head, I cross out the number five next to it and move it up the list to the number one spot. "Good day?" I try to ask casually, but it comes out all squeaky like that mouse I rescued. Dad doesn't notice.

"Not bad. They got the broken computers at the job centre fixed, so the queue for them wasn't as long today, at least."

I try to think of a way to lead up to my question like we just stumbled onto the subject naturally, but my mind's gone blank and I just blurt it out. "Dad, was I really grown in a test tube in a lab, or do I have a real mum somewhere?"

"What?" The glass of water Dad poured himself stops halfway to his mouth. He blinks at me, and I can see frown lines forming above his eyes. "What made you think about that?" he asks suspiciously.

"Um…there were just some kids at school talking about it last week, that's all. They said you have to have a mother to be born, and everyone's got one."

"Oh, just some kids talking." Dad's face relaxes a bit, and he takes a big gulp of water. "What do kids know about the wonders of science? You were mixed up in a test tube and grown in a lab, and then when you were big enough I got to take you home with me."

His grin is real enough, but there's something not right about his eyes.

"Is that really true?" I ask. It's something I've never said to Dad before, and I search his face, trying to read the story hidden there. Dad turns away and opens the cupboard, pulling out the milkshake powder and taking a bottle of milk from the fridge. "Course it is. You're my little Sunny Day, full of banana sunshine, aren't you? Here, have a glass just now. Ed got his benefits today, so he promised to go shopping and bring back a takeaway tonight. It shouldn't be too long now till dinner."

I hope not. There's nothing in the cupboards, and my belly's been rumbling since that bowl of cereal I had at breakfast. Dad's just handing me the glass when Ed walks in. He's a mean-faced little man with greasy hair and wrinkled skin who looks like he's been left out to dry in the sun for too long. He scowls as soon as he sees we've used up the last of the milk.

"Eating again? Jeez, Ronnie, I can't afford this. Money for food doesn't grow on trees."

"I know, Ed," Dad says. "I bought that milk, just like I've bought all the groceries since we arrived. Did you get the shopping like you promised?" Dad's voice is calm, but I can see his jaw clenching like he's annoyed.

Ed doesn't answer the question straight, like he would've done if he wasn't trying to hide something. "How am I meant to feed all these extra mouths, Ronnie? Hard times, it is. Hard times."

"I paid you two weeks' rent up front, that's how," Dad says, his voice getting harder, like it does when he argues with hostel managers or staff down at the job centre when his benefits have been cut. "Are you telling me it's gone on the horses again and there's nothing for the kids' dinner?"

"Get off my case, Ronnie," Ed snaps, rummaging in the cupboard for the last bag of crisps. "I've had a long day."

"A long day throwing all the food money away?" Dad's sounding angry for real now, and his jaw's clenching so hard I'm scared his teeth are going to break. "For God's sake, Ed, how are we meant to feed—"

"Not in front of the kid, alright?" Ed growls, throwing me a look that says it's all my fault just for being there. "Let's take this outside, OK? I need a smoke anyway."

"Right, so you've got money for cigarettes, just not for..." Dad's voice fades as the front door slams behind him. I'm left standing there in the kitchen holding a glass of milkshake that I feel really bad for drinking even though Dad paid for it. I'm thirsty, though, and if there's nothing else in the house, then this'll have to do me for dinner. I take a sip, but the milkshake doesn't taste like sunshine today; it tastes like a sky full of rain clouds and dark secrets.

Chapter 10

ADAM

I don't get why my mother won't admit that she really misses her old job and just go back to work. Her endless projects to fill her spare time in between fussing over me and cooking and cleaning are taking over the whole kitchen.

Today she's making soup for the church coffee club. For most normal people, that would involve a couple of large pots, a chopping board and a big bowl of vegetables. It would take maybe an hour. But my mother never does anything by halves, and her soup needs a mountain of carrots, parsnips, and onions that cover every available surface, giant pots on every gas ring, three chopping boards, and every knife and spoon we own. She's already used up all of our food waste bags, and she still has another two buckets of carrots to peel.

"I'm off to work on my project up in the treehouse," I call over the hiss of bubbling pots. "I'll be back for dinner. I'll put these bags in the food bin outside."

Mum looks up from her chopping board in alarm. "Just leave them, Adam, they're too heavy for you."

"Mum, they're just vegetable peelings!" I roll my eyes. "I'm not a total wimp!" I wish she would stop treating me like I'm a fragile piece of glass that'll break if the wind blows too hard. I pick the bags up and carry them out the door to show her I can manage, but luckily the windows are all steamed up with boiling pots so she can't watch what I get up to out here.

I've just dumped the last bag in the food bin when a loud knocking at the back gate carries all the way across the garden. I get such a fright I forget to close the bin lid, racing across the lawn to stop the knocking before my mother hears it above all the cooking sounds in the kitchen.

"Stop knocking!" I whisper, "or my mother will hear you!"

The knocking stops at once, but when I open the gate, Norah's on the other side frowning at me. "How come you don't want her to know about me?" she pouts. "Are you ashamed to be seen with me? Cos if you are, I can find someone else to hang out with."

"Of course not!" I close the gate quickly, but shutting her out of my garden just makes her frown harder.

"Whatever," she mutters, stomping back through the trees to retrieve her bike.

"Norah, it's not like that!" I chase after her, and when we get to the path, I grab her arm before she can cycle off. "My parents are just crazy strict, that's all," I say. I don't want to tell her about my cancer. I don't want her feeling sorry for me or thinking I'm infectious or something, so I tell a half-lie instead. "I'm supposed to be working all Easter in my treehouse on a project about climate change. If my mother finds out I haven't been studying there, I'll be in big trouble."

"Oh," Norah says quietly, fiddling with the handlebars on her bike. It takes me a second to realise this isn't really about me after all. There's something else bothering her. She looks really tired, and even though her jeans and T-shirt are clean for once, they're all rumpled like they've not been dried on a washing line or ironed like my clothes.

"So…did you have a tough time babysitting?" I try, pulling my hood up again as we pass the crowds round the swings.

"Urgh, the *worst*!" Norah finally lifts her head and looks straight at me, and I know I've found the problem.

"What happened? Did the kids turn into gremlins the minute their parents' backs were turned?"

"What's a gremlin?"

Oh, I forgot. The rest of the world doesn't spend all of their time locked in the house watching old films because they ran out of new things to watch in the hospital. "Sort of like…monsters," I tell her. "They look cute at first, but then they turn really nasty and cause loads of trouble."

"That's *exactly* what they are!" Norah nods. "They're *gremlins*." She starts pedalling and I have to jog to keep up. "Danny's the worst, cos he's the cutest, and he knows it. When his mum's away he just goes wild—climbing over everything and then screaming when he doesn't get his own way. Or maybe Chris is the worst cos he's the oldest and should be helping me with them, but he just winds his brothers and sister up and makes them cry. Toby does *everything* Chris tells him to do—he covered the bathroom floor with a whole tube of Frost Fresh toothpaste cos Chris said it would be like an ice rink. It wasn't. It was like a hundred pigeons had pooped in there at once, and I had to clean it up. Baby Mikie cries all night, and that sets little Kayla off, and…" Norah runs out of breath and just shakes her head.

"Are you staying with your cousins over Easter, then?" I ask.

"Uh, yeah, with my…Uncle Ed and Aunt Cheryl. And Cheryl's brother. And Dad, of course. It's not a very big flat, so we're all squashed in like too many baked beans in a can."

"Wow. Sounds…pretty crazy." I meant to sound sympathetic, but it comes out sounding envious. My grandparents died when I was little, and I've just got one aunt way up in the north of Scotland. Now that I don't have any friends anymore either, every weekend and holiday it's just the three of us here in Hull. I didn't realise how empty that made me feel until I met Norah.

"Must be nice, living somewhere so quiet in such a big house," Norah says.

"Um, yeah, it's OK," I shrug. She shoots me a funny look, but doesn't say anything more about it.

The nature trail's even quieter today, and even the park's half empty, but I think that's because a new funfair just opened on the other side of the city. I saw an advert for it in the local paper and I cut it out and stuck it on the fridge next to the swimming pool leaflet I put up ages ago, but my mother pretends she can't see either of them.

We sit down on the log at the little clearing where we left the robins, and I pull out a bag full of seeds, nuts and berries. It was all I managed to collect before my mother took over the kitchen to make her soup, and I didn't want to make her suspicious by packing a picnic. When I see the disappointment in Norah's eyes, I wish I'd just risked it and brought food anyway.

"Sorry, this is all I had time to get."

"That's great," Norah says too quickly. "The birds will love it."

We scatter some of the berries and seeds on the ground and wait, but the robins don't come. Sitting there, staring up into the branches and trying to pretend I don't notice Norah's slipping her hand into the bag and stuffing fistfuls of nuts and berries into her mouth like she hasn't eaten in days, I start feeling awkward. This day isn't turning out like I planned. I've already made Norah think that I don't want her in my garden, even though I wish I could play on the swings with her and show her the goldfish in the pond. Now I've made her think that I'm too selfish to bring a packed lunch, even though I've clearly got loads of food in my house. She probably won't want to hang out with me again after today.

"Maybe we should—" I start to say, when Norah mumbles, "Shh!" through a mouthful of nuts. There's a rustle in the bushes, and suddenly a grey blur streaks across the ground and starts shoving nuts into its mouth even faster than Norah did. A few seconds later more squirrels come scurrying down a tree trunk, stopping to sniff the air before running over to grab the rest of the seeds and berries. These ones are only half size, and they're even braver than the adult one. When they finish what's on the ground they come climbing right up our legs in search of more.

Norah and I split the bag, holding the food out for the squirrels and grinning at each other. This is better than the funfair, and way better than the zoo my parents took me to when I was little.

"Maybe we could keep them in your treehouse?" Norah says eagerly. "You've got a big garden for them to run around, and we could—"

"They don't need rescued, Norah!" I laugh. "They're happy here."

"But they look really hungry!"

"Greedy, more like. And anyway, I've got that stupid cat hanging around trying to eat the wildlife, remember?"

Norah's face falls. She's even more desperate for a pet than I am, which is odd seeing as she has so many cousins to love.

"We can't take them away from their home," I say, trying to convince her that adopting a family of squirrels isn't a good idea. "How would you like it if someone came and took you away from your home when you didn't want them to?"

The look Norah gives me makes me see straight away I've said the wrong thing. She gulps hard and looks away. "Not everyone has a home," she mutters.

"You mean you don't…?"

"Course I do!" she snaps. "I just meant…I found a dog last weekend. He was starving and all grubby, and nobody wanted him except me. I called him Bingo, and he followed me home, but Dad said I couldn't keep him, and we left him behind when we went to Uncle Ed's. He's probably died of hunger, or been hit by a car or—"

"Or maybe he'll be sitting outside your house waiting for you when you go home after the holidays," I say cheerfully, trying to make her smile again.

It doesn't work. Norah throws me another look that says I just don't get it. We go back to watching the squirrels, but they disappear as soon as the food's gone. I wish I could think of something else to say to Norah, but it's like we're both hiding secrets we don't want to share, and I'm scared to ask her any more questions in case I say the wrong thing again. Luckily Norah breaks the silence before it gets too uncomfortable.

"So, it's your turn," she says, wiping her fingers on her jeans and getting them covered in berry stains.

"For what?"

"To tell me about yourself. I told you about babysitting the gremlins, and about Bingo, so you need to tell me something."

"Um…" I shuffle on the log nervously. I don't want Norah to know how weird my life is in case she thinks I'm a freak. "Like what?"

"Like what you do in that big house at the weekend, and where you go to school and if your family's nice or not. Like why you can't have another pet even though you had a dog before, or why you pull your hood up when you pass people like you're ashamed to be seen with me. Like why you can't have friends over. And don't say it's cos your parents are strict or you're supposed to be studying, cos I know when you're lying. It's me, isn't it? You don't want me in your nice house or want your nice mum and dad to know that a nice boy like you is hanging around with someone like me."

Norah's bottom lip's wobbling, and I have no idea what to say to make it stop.

Just then I'm saved. The sky's been getting darker all afternoon, and now it opens up, big drops of rain splashing down through the trees.

"I've got to get back," I say quickly. "My mother will know I wasn't studying in the treehouse if I come back all wet. You'd better go home too before you're soaked."

Norah's only got a thin jacket on over her T-shirt, and it looks like she grew out of it ages ago as it's too small for her to zip up. She nods sadly, like she knows the fun we had with the squirrels was too good to last.

We hurry back through the nature trail to the gate before the rain gets too heavy. The park's starting to empty, everyone scurrying home to get out of the downpour.

Before Norah can cycle away I call, "Do you want to meet up again? I'll bring a picnic next time—promise!"

Norah stops and looks back. "You want to hang out with me again?"

"Of course! We're the animal rescue team, remember?" I try not to make it sound like I'm too eager, but if she says no, then I'm going to have to walk away so she doesn't see how bad it would make me feel. She doesn't say no. She smiles and says, "Can we make it Monday?"

"You babysitting till then?"

Norah makes a face.

"Alright," I laugh, relieved. "Two o'clock still OK? And don't knock this time!"

Norah throws me a salute that has me laughing again, and cycles off with her head down against the wind. I run the other way, hoping my mother will believe I got this wet just climbing down from the treehouse.

When I get back to the garden, the kitchen windows are even more steamed up than when I left, but what makes me stop dead is the sight of the rubbish that's strewn all across the patio. I forgot to shut the food waste bin, and the neighbour's ginger cat has pulled out all the bags and ripped them to shreds. She's rummaging in the last one, searching for scraps to eat, when I run up to her so fast she jumps in fright and knocks over the empty bin trying to get away. I'm even angrier with her than usual. She's already eaten two of my father's fish this week, and I'm sick of her spoiling my garden.

My mother opens the back door and puts her head out when she hears the noise. "Adam!" she gasps, "you're soaking wet! You'll catch a chill!"

"It's just rain, Mum," I grumble as she pulls me inside and starts towelling me off like I've been dunked in a bucket of water instead of just a few drops.

"You need to get out of those clothes," she fusses, not listening. "Remember what the doctors said about keeping warm?"

That was when I was sick with cancer and hooked up to machines in the hospital! I want to yell at her. I'm so tired of all her drama. I can't be bothered to argue, though.

"Fine, I'll get changed after I put the bags back in the food bin," I sigh. I feel a bit bad about the mess—I was the one who forgot to lock the lid, and my mother has enough pots and pans to wash in the kitchen to last her till midnight.

"I'll get those, just go and dry off before you catch a cold," she says, vigorously towelling my hair that's already bone dry since my hood was up.

"But the cat—"

"Don't worry about the cat. I've been meaning to call the animal shelter about her and have her collected."

"Why?" I grab the towel off my mother before she can rub a hole right through my scalp. "Shouldn't you talk to the neighbours about her first? The shelter might put her down."

"They moved to Italy last month and left her behind," she tuts. "The house hasn't been sold yet, but I don't think the next people who live there will want a stray cat rummaging around in their bins any more than I do. Would you like me to run you a bath? A nice hot bath before dinner would do you good."

"I'm fine." I'm hurrying to the door before she insists on wrapping me up in cotton wool, when something makes me stop.

I *hate* that cat. She's an evil menace.

But she's been abandoned.

She's eaten the baby robin's parents. And my father's fish.

But she's hungry.

Yeah, but I *hate* cats…

"Mum," I hear myself saying before I even realise what I'm doing, "Couldn't we adopt her? I mean, if she doesn't have anyone else to look after her, then—"

"Go and get some dry clothes, Adam," my mother says, her lips drawn into a thin line. "I'll come up in a minute and run you a bath."

There's just no point arguing with her. I drag my feet all the way up the stairs, trying to remind myself how much I hate that ginger cat and pretending not to worry that the rain's coming down hard against the windows and she's got no home to go to.

Chapter 11

NORAH

I'm crying so hard I can barely see straight. Dad grabs me by the arms and half lifts me out of the front door and into the hall before I can shriek the place down.

"Calm down, Norah," he soothes, "it was just an accident."

"It wasn't!" I wail. "Chris did it on purpose! I saw him! He squashed Boris flat just because I wouldn't let him pull Kayla's hair!"

"It was just a spider, pet," Dad sighs. "You can't expect other people to—"

"He was *my* spider! He was the only thing I had left, and Chris killed him for nothing! I *hate* him and the stupid gremlins, and I *hate* it here! I want to go *home*!" It's not fair saying all this to Dad when there's nothing he can do about it, but I'm so upset it comes tumbling out before I can stop it.

Dad gives me a big hug until I calm down and stop gulping like I'm drowning. "I know it's tough, pet," he says, "but it's not for much longer. I got some good news this morning. D'you want to hear it? Hmm?"

I stop sniffing and lift my head off his chest to look at him. "What is it?"

Dad grins, a proper happy smile that fills me with hope. "The good news is I've got a job!"

"Really?" If Dad's just trying to make me feel better about Boris, then it's working. He hasn't had a job in nearly six months, so this is the best news *ever*! "What are you going to be doing? It's not another leaflet delivery job, is it? The pay was rubbish for the last one."

"No, it's packing in a warehouse—a bit like what I was doing before, when we lived in Ash Lane, remember?"

Only *a bit* like it? That makes me suspicious. Dad was a supervisor before the company went bust and we lost our home, and he was in charge of lots of people. He'd had that job since he left school, and the manager made sure he had help reading anything that was written down. Dad always said his old boss was one in a million. I bet now he's starting right at the bottom all over again on less money. But I've got a way more important question to ask than that one. "Is it full time?"

Dad's smile slips a bit. "Maybe down the road, pet. I'm sure I'll get plenty of hours, though, so don't worry about it."

"*Dad*!" I know exactly what that means. It's a zero hours contract, so he won't get definite hours to do and he won't know from week to week how much he'll earn. He'll just have to wait around every day for them to call him in, even though some days they won't call him at all.

"I can't help it, Norah. That's all that was going, and it pays a bit better than the benefits. Once I've saved up some pay cheques, we'll start looking for somewhere to rent. That sounds good, doesn't it?"

I nod, trying to look enthusiastic. It does sound good, but I've heard the same thing too many times before to really get my hopes up. It's always the same: Dad gets a job, he saves up some money, we start looking for a place to rent, and life looks sunny again. But then the work dries up and Dad's laid off, and the job centre makes a mistake with the benefits, or a hostel says we owe them rent. Then not only does he not have a job anymore, but we don't have any money either and no place to stay that isn't a homeless hostel or a B&B. One time we got so close to renting a place we were standing in the estate agents waiting to sign the papers, but then they said they couldn't give us the house as Dad's credit checks had failed cos he'd been on benefits, and we didn't know anyone with a good credit score who could sign the papers for us. I'm rubbish at maths and spelling, but I know everything there is to know about how hard it is to get a proper job and get off benefits for good. Dad's zero hours isn't my biggest worry right now, though.

"If you've got a job, then social services can't take me away, can they?" I ask anxiously, trying to read his face through a big blur of tears.

"What? Of course they can't, pet, that's never going to happen."

"But I saw you talking to that woman in the library, she said—"

"I told you; she was just someone who thought I'd skipped the computer queue, that's all. Social services haven't contacted me, so you've got nothing to worry about. And now

I've got a job, they can't say I'm not looking after you, can they? It's going to turn out right this time, you'll see." Dad gives me another squeeze. "You believe me, don't you, Sunny?"

I try to give him the smile he's looking for, but it's fake. I don't believe him anymore. It was OK when he was just lying to make me feel better about him not being hungry and about Santa. But now he's lying to me about gambling on the horses when he's supposed to be filling in job search forms, about social services calling, and about whether I've got a mother. I don't know what to believe anymore. I'm too scared to ask Dad about all that, though. I'm too scared to know the truth.

Just then, Cheryl's brother, Jim, and Ed come up the stairs. They both smell like beer and stale smoke, and Ed's got that hungry look in his eyes that says he's after more than food. "Ronnie!" He gives Dad a gap-toothed grin when he sees him. "Just the man. Heard you got yourself a cushy little job down at the Dobson's warehouse. Reckon that means you can afford to pay for all the electricity and heating you and your kid have been using all week, eh?"

Dad's smile vanishes and he scowls at Ed. "We already agreed a price, and I paid you last week," he mutters. "I've paid double in food for everyone as it is."

"Circumstances change," Ed sniggers, and Jim gives a mean laugh that comes out his nose instead of his mouth. "Come inside and we'll discuss the new charges."

Dad storms into the flat after them, and I'm left standing in the hall on my own. I want to believe Dad when he says everything is OK, but I've got a big secret burning a hole in my pocket that says it won't. I pull out the card that I've Sellotaped back together and take another look at it.

Sandra Gibson. Rainbow Children's Centre, Grimsby.

There's no way a random woman arguing over a computer would give him a business card. There's no way the "Rainbow Children's Centre" is anything other than a social services care home. And there's no way I'm going to get any of the answers I need from Dad.

"Norah, get in here, will you?" Ed shouts from the flat so loud all the neighbours can hear. "Cheryl needs help with the kids."

No chance. I've already been locked in this prison with those evil brats all weekend, and I'm so tired of breaking up fights and cleaning up after everyone I could scream. I grab my bike from behind the door and clomp down the stairs with it before anyone can stop me. I promised Adam I'd meet him in the park, and that's one thing I'm not going to lie to him about.

I cycle by the rows of flats with clapped-out cars and overflowing rubbish bins outside, down the alley covered in graffiti and empty beer cans, and out to the main road that winds past the run-down shops all the way to the posher bit of town. I try not to think about poor Boris, or Dad's lies, and focus on all the good stuff instead. Dad's got a job, which is great, even if it probably won't last as it's just a rubbish zero hours one. I've still got another week off school, which means I won't have to see Chelsea Mackay and her mean gang till next Monday. And best of all, Adam still wants to see me even though I wasn't very friendly last time.

I didn't mean to act all grumpy, but there wasn't any money for dinner the night before and I was really hungry. I hoped he was going to bring a picnic like last time, but now he probably thinks I'm just using him to get food off him like I'm a stray dog or something.

Talking of stray dogs...

I slow down as I pass the old bingo hall, my chest tightening with the hope I'm trying to swallow down in case I'm disappointed. I check the bins behind the alley, but the little Highland terrier isn't there. The hall must've been a cinema years ago, as it's got a big fancy front entrance. I go up the steps and try to peer into the ticket hall. One of the boards across the bottom of the smashed glass door is loose, and I can lift it up to peer inside. I can't see much, though, just darkness and dust and emptiness. The dog isn't here. I guess I didn't really expect him to be, but it still makes my heart sink to the bottom of my shoes.

An old woman tuts as she walks past, and a group of teenagers all laugh when they see me, and I finally work out that crouching on the steps staring into an abandoned building and yelling "Bingo!" at the top of my voice probably makes me look like a crazy person. I grab my bike and cycle away quick before the high school kids start taking pictures of me to post on the Internet.

By the time I get to the park, the sky's looking grey again and I'm worried Adam won't come out in case it rains. He was pretty worried about getting wet last time, and I don't want him to run off before we've had time to talk. I might tell him the truth about where I live. I want Adam to be my friend, and friends don't lie to each other, do they?

Not like Dad.

I remember not to knock on the gate, but even if I hadn't it wouldn't matter, cos it's Adam who's waiting for me this time.

"I thought you weren't coming!" he says, a big grin on his face as he closes the gate behind him. He's happy to see me, and that makes me feel like today might turn out to be a banana sunshine day after all despite the grey clouds.

"Sorry I'm late, I was babysitting the gremlins again." I make a face and he laughs. He's got a nice laugh, not like Ed or Cheryl's brother.

"How come your aunt and uncle are making you babysit your cousins all holiday?" he asks. "Are they working all day?"

I bite my lip, but then I decide to tell him the truth. "They're not my real aunt and uncle, they're just people we're staying with as we got kicked out of our bed and breakfast cos we couldn't pay the rent."

"Oh." Adam blinks, trying to work out what that means. "So you were staying at a B&B for the Easter holidays? I thought you lived in Hull?"

He's not getting it, and I have to spell it out for him even though I'm rubbish at spelling. "I do live in Hull, but Dad lost his job a couple of years ago and we couldn't pay the rent anymore. We didn't have anywhere to live, so the council have been moving us to different hostels and B&Bs since then. We can't get anything permanent cos it costs too much."

I don't want to use the word "homeless". It's like a label someone at the stupid housing office attached to me without my permission, and if I say it out loud, then that might make it stick on permanently.

"Oh," Adam says again. I wish he wouldn't. It makes it sound like my life's too weird for him to wrap his head around. "Can't your dad get another job?"

I grit my teeth, trying to stay patient, but, wow, doesn't he know *anything*? "It's not that easy. The only jobs he can get are rubbish zero hours ones that always finish after a few months, and then we're back to where we started."

"But couldn't he work in an office? My dad's a lawyer for a big company—maybe if I asked him he might be able to find a job for—"

"Don't be so stupid!" I don't mean to snap, but Adam's starting to make me regret telling him the truth. "Not everyone did well at school and went to university! Not everyone can get nice office jobs and live in posh houses with big gardens and fancy treehouses. Not everyone has legs the length of double-decker buses and can 'Stand Up and Stand Out' in their expensive clothes!"

That last bit just slipped out. Adam's wearing the same T-shirt I saw on that bus advert, but if I try to explain that to him now he'll think I'm totally off my head. He's not looking at me like I'm mad, though. He's just looking worried about me.

"I'm sorry," he says quietly, "I didn't mean to upset you. It sounds really tough."

I shrug, trying to make it look like it doesn't bother me. "It's fine, so don't feel sorry for me, OK?"

"OK, as long as you don't feel sorry for me either."

"Why would I ever feel sorry for *you*?" It's my turn to blink at him like he's lost it.

Adam just shrugs and starts walking across the park. I cycle after him when I see him putting up an umbrella just in case it rains. That means he's not planning on running off if the clouds don't behave themselves. I'm just about to ask him how his school project's going, when he catches sight of someone passing with a small kid and he pulls the hood of his jacket up and turns his face away.

That does it. I'm so tired of this. I roll my bike up to the side up of the duck pond and sit down on the grass. I'm on strike until he tells me what's going on. Adam finally figures out that I'm not following him anymore and comes over, looking round nervously to see if anyone's watching us.

"I thought we were going to the nature trail?" he says.

"Maybe. That depends."

"On what?"

"On you telling me the truth. I'm sick of everyone lying to me. Why do you keep pulling your hood up and hiding from people? Are you scared of been seen with me in case your posh friends all laugh at you?"

Adam heaves a big sigh and pulls his hood down again. "Sorry, it's just…I'm not scared to be seen with you, I'm just scared to be *seen*. If my mother knew I was out of the garden on my own, she'd go crazy."

"You're not on your own, you're with me," I point out.

"I mean without her."

"She doesn't let you go anywhere without her?"

"She doesn't let me go *anywhere*!" Adam mutters. "Ever since…" He stops and looks away, but I don't push him. I just wait till he's ready. When he turns back, he's looking at the ducks playing in the water and his eyes are really sad. "I used to love the water," he says softly. "I used to go to the swimming club every day after school when we lived in Durham. I won the North East Regional Championships for under tens twice, and I've got loads of medals and two big trophies."

"You're not from Hull?"

"No, we moved here so I could try a new cancer treatment. Can't you tell from my accent?"

"Oh, I thought that's just how posh people talked." I hurry on before Adam thinks I'm a moron. "So why did you stop swimming?"

Adam picks at the grass, pulling the petals off a dandelion angrily. "I got sick. Leukaemia. It's a type of cancer. I was in and out of the hospital for ages. I lost my hair, and even though I threw up a lot, the drugs made me put on a lot of weight. I got really weak, and it was dangerous for me to go outside in case I caught any germs."

"But you're better now?" I try not to sound worried, but Adam hears my voice go all high pitched and he smiles like he's happy I care.

"My cancer's in remission—that means it's gone, hopefully for good. I still have to take pills every day and have treatment at the clinic once a month, but as far as my mother's concerned, it's like nothing's changed. She still treats me like I'm so fragile I'm going to break any second, and she won't let me leave the house and garden. She even got me a private tutor so I can't go back to school. You're the first person I've talked to other than him and my parents in about a billion years."

"Oh." It's my turn to say it now. "That really sucks."

"Yeah. But it's fine since I've got a posh house with a big garden and a fancy treehouse and legs the length of a double-decker bus, so don't feel sorry for me, OK?"

He gives me a look that says he's kidding, and I burst out laughing. I was wrong about Adam. Our lives are totally different, but neither of them are perfect.

We sit watching the ducks mucking about on the water for a while, then Adam pulls out a bag of breadcrumbs. "You want to feed the ducks?

Then we can go to the nature trail and look for animals to rescue. I brought some sausage rolls left over from lunch and some Mars bars in case we get hungry."

I grin at that and exchange high fives with him.

Today is most definitely going to be a banana sunshine day after all.

I'm just reaching into the bag of crumbs to feed the ducks when I hear a nasty laugh behind me.

"Hey, look! Norah-the-homeless-tramp's found a boyfriend and he's feeding her scraps from his bin!"

I turn round, my heart beating fast. Chelsea Mackay's stomping up the path towards me, and she's got two of her biggest, meanest foster brothers with her.

Chapter 12

ADAM

As soon as Norah sees the girl coming up the path, she backs away, but there's nowhere to go as the pond is right behind her.

"Do you know these kids?" I ask quietly, but Norah doesn't answer. Her face has gone tight with fear, and that makes my stomach clench too. The girl looks really tough, but it's the mean look in the older boys' eyes that worries me the most.

"What are you doing in my park, Norah no-mates?" the girl sneers, shoving her face right up to Norah so she can't look away. "Didn't you see the 'No Homeless' sign?"

"It's not your park!" Norah says bravely, even though her voice is shaking. "I've never seen you here before."

"What did you say? Are you talking to me, you smelly tramp?" The girl's cheeks are going red with anger, and she's standing so close I can smell her expensive perfume. It's the same kind my mother wears, but somehow there's a sour note underneath like it's been sitting in the shop display for too long and has gone off.

Before Norah can reply, one of the boys takes hold of her bike, pulling it from her. She lunges for it, but all she can get hold of is the light at the front before it's wrenched out of reach. It breaks off in her hand and falls on the grass, and she's left staring down at it in shock.

"Nice wheels," the boy sniggers. "What are you, three years old? What kind of loser needs stabilisers?"

"Give that back, it's mine!" Norah yells.

Before she can snatch her bike back again, the other boy grabs her arms. "Hey, Nate, wouldn't your little sister like a bike like this one?"

The first boy grins. "Yeah, she would. Reckon this'll do a treat for her birthday. You want a ride home, Chelsea?" The smirking girl sits in the saddle even though it's way too small for her, and the boy starts wheeling the bike away. "Thanks, kid. See you."

That's when Norah goes completely nuts.

"Give it back!" she shrieks. "You can't take it!" She tries to kick the boy who's still holding her arms, but he's way too big for her, and he swipes her legs out from under her. She goes tumbling down onto the path, scraping her hand on the stones. When she hunches over, cradling it to her chest, I can see blood running from the cut down the side of her palm. That finally wakes me. Up till now I've been frozen in fear, and it's like I've been watching the whole thing on TV rather than in real life.

I feel a jolt of electricity running through me, and before I know what I'm doing I launch myself at the boy, swinging a punch out of nowhere. It catches him on the side of the chin and he staggers back, stunned for a second. But even though I'm tall for my age, I'm still younger, and the boy's got shoulders like a sumo wrestler. He charges at me and shoves me so hard my feet leave the ground. I'm flying back, back…then suddenly there's a huge splash and the world goes dark.

I get such a fright that for a second, I don't know where I am. The water's cold and deep, and as it closes over my head, I can't help taking a breath. The pain when it shoots down my nose and burns all the way to my lungs stops me thinking straight. I've been underwater a million times before. I used to be able to swim better than almost anyone my age I've ever met. But it's been so long since I've been in the pool that I've lost all my confidence. I was a champion swimmer before I got sick, but I'm scared the chemicals the doctors pumped me full of are like Superman's kryptonite. Maybe now I don't know how to swim anymore. Maybe I'm going to drown.

I thrash around in panic when I realise the pond's too deep for my feet to touch the bottom, swallowing another mouthful of water. It's only when my flailing hands catch hold of the bricks round the edge that I manage to haul myself up, gasping and choking as I surface again. It takes a full minute for my heart to stop hammering and for my eyes to clear. When the world comes into focus, I can see Norah still sitting in a crumpled ball on the path, cradling her hand, and the silver stripes on her bike flashing behind the park railings as the group of kids disappear down the road. That isn't what makes me feel sick to my stomach, though.

My mother's running across the park, and even though I've got water in my ears, I can hear her yelling my name like the whole world is ending.

I scramble out of the pond and onto the grass, but even though Norah's hurt way worse than I am, my mother scoops me up like no one else in the world even exists. "Adam, what happened?" she cries, all the fear and terror I saw in the hospital back in her eyes. Before I can answer, she's pulling her cardigan off and wrapping it round my shoulders, and I'm too shocked by what happened and frightened by her overreaction to complain she's making me look like an old woman.

"Wait!" I cough as she tries to lead me away. "Norah's hurt!"

"Norah who…?" My mother catches sight of the girl on the path, and she hesitates for a second before letting go of me and bending down to check on her. "Oh, I've seen you at church and at the foodbank. Are you alright?" she asks. "Where are your parents? They should take you home and get that cut washed."

Norah's crying too hard to reply. I think she's more upset about her stolen bike than the fact her hand's bleeding, though.

I cough up another mouthful of water and croak, "Her dad's at work. We need to take her back to our house to clean her hand."

My mother purses her lips. "I need to get you dry, Adam. It would be better if Norah went to her own home and—"

"Mum!" I gasp. I can't believe she's being this selfish. Just because she thinks the whole world revolves around me doesn't make it a scientific fact. I'm not sure if my mother realises she's wrong, or whether she just agrees to help Norah to shut me up and get me back home as fast as possible. Either way, she helps Norah to her feet, and with one hand on her arm and the other round my shoulder, leads us back to the house.

When we get to the fence, I see the back gate's hanging open. I mustn't have closed it properly. That must be how my mother knew I wasn't in the treehouse. I'm such an idiot.

The next hour passes in a blur.

My mother insists on running me a hot bath before she bandages Norah's hand, and while I'm washing all the pond water out of my hair, she calls Norah's dad even though Norah asks her not to. I don't think Norah's scared she's going to get in trouble when her dad comes. I think she's scared her dad's going to be in trouble with my mother when he comes for leaving Norah in the park on her own.

My mother comes back with a hot water bottle and wraps me in the fluffiest bath towel she can find. She makes me go straight to bed, which is mad as it's only three o'clock, but when there's a knock at the front door, I sneak out and sit at the top of the stairs to listen to the angry voices below.

"I'm calling the police!" my mother cries, sounding all strung out like she's just drunk ten cups of strong coffee in a row. "Those boys could have killed Adam!"

There's a low rumbling that must be Norah's father trying to calm her down, and then my mother's voice cuts the air like a knife again.

"What do you mean they were 'just messing about'? They stole your daughter's bicycle and nearly drowned my son!"

The rumbling sounds lower, apologetic, and I can hear my mother tutting over the top of it.

"She let her friends borrow her bike? That's not what Adam said. He said—"

This time I can hear Norah's dad's voice getting louder. "I'm sorry Adam fell in the pond, but it was just kids mucking around like Norah said, OK? No harm done. Norah knows the other kids, and she's happy for them to play with her bike, aren't you, pet?"

There's a funny little noise that sounds like a whimper, and then Norah's dad's talking again.

"There's no point wasting police time over this. Thanks for looking after Norah, I appreciate it. I'll take her home now."

"I shouldn't have had to look after her. You should have been in the park with her, not leaving her all on her own!"

"I know how to look after my own daughter, thanks. She's eleven years old, she's not a baby, and she wasn't on her own, was she? She was playing with your son." Norah's dad sounds angry, like he's biting his tongue to stop himself saying what he really thinks.

"Well, that's the last time I want her anywhere near Adam," my mother snaps. "He's never been disobedient before. Norah's a bad influence. Keep a closer eye on her in future, and don't let her come back here disturbing my son."

"Fine by me." Norah's dad's voice is so tense it's like a piano string that's ready to snap. Instead of a loud twang there's a crash, and that's the front door slamming. Norah and her dad are gone, and I hurry back to bed before my mother catches me disobeying her again. There's no point breaking the rules—today's proved that it's just not worth it. If only I'd done what I was told and stayed in the garden right from the start, then none of this would ever have happened.

My mother comes up a minute later with a mug of hot chocolate. It's sweet and comforting, and I let her fuss over me and bring me my favourite comics like she did when I was in hospital. It's much easier just giving in to her. That way she won't be angry with me. That way she'll stop looking worried and smile at me instead. I let her comb my hair even though I haven't let her do that since I was about eight, and I let her tuck me in and bring me biscuits even though a few days ago all the fussing would've driven me mad.

"I'll bring your dinner up on a tray," she tells me. "We can watch some films on your computer afterwards, OK?"

I nod and smile. It's not a real smile, but it doesn't matter. What's the point in me telling the truth about anything anymore? Norah didn't. Norah said those kids were her friends and they were just having fun, and that made me look like a liar in front of my mother. If Norah doesn't even care enough about me or her bike to call the police and report them, then there's no point in me caring about her stupid bike either. Caring about people just gets you hurt. There's no point in caring about anything anymore. Better just to stay here in my room where it's warm and safe and my mother will bring me hot chocolate and biscuits whenever I want.

My mother must've called my father about what happened, as he comes home really early. He's in time for dinner for the first time in forever, and since I'm still in bed, my mother brings everything up to my room on trays. We sit around eating together like it's a picnic, and Dad tells me about his day at work and about the fox he saw running through the car park outside his office even though it's in the middle of the city. He hasn't spoken to me properly about anything in ages, and it makes me feel all warm inside that he remembers how much I like hearing about animals. He helps my mother take all the dinner things back down to the kitchen, and I think he's going to spend the rest of the evening in his office working, but he comes back up right away.

"You're OK, aren't you, Adam?" he asks, flicking through the books on my bookshelf and trying to pretend there's a reason for him to be back in here instead of working.

"Yeah, Dad, I'm fi—" I start to say, but then I remember what happened when my cancer went into remission and I didn't have to be in hospital all the time. My father stopped reading me stories and sitting with me at bedtime. He stopped eating dinner with me and my mother and stayed up late working instead. I don't want things to go back to the way they were when he thought I was fine.

"I've got a really sore throat," I say instead, coughing hard to prove it, even though I've swallowed way more swimming pool water during training sessions. "My head hurts too." It's not really a lie. My head does feel a bit fuzzy after everything that's happened today.

Dad picks up the book I'm halfway through reading and comes to sit on my bed. He has to move a lot of my stuffed animals to clear a space, but that's OK as I hate them anyway.

"Do you want me to read to you for a bit?" he offers.

I nod. I want that more than anything.

I thought I wanted my parents to realise I was well more than anything, but I was wrong. My life's much better when I'm sick. I don't want to be well ever again.

Chapter 13

NORAH

"And my mum sent me these amazing jeans too—did you see my jeans, Yasmin?" Chelsea Mackay opens her school bag again so the kids at the table opposite can see the designer label. We've been back at school for over two weeks and Chelsea still hasn't shut up about all the expensive stuff her mum sent her from New York over the holidays.

I keep my head down and go back to colouring in all the things on my worksheet beginning with the letter "b". It's baby stuff I can do in my sleep, but the Year Six teacher doesn't know what to do with the kids from the special class when we're supposed to join the mainstreamers for science, so he just dumps us at our own table and gives us coloured pens. Chelsea's the only one who can talk to the mainstream kids without them laughing at her. It's like her mum's fancy presents give her a superpower or something.

I can't help wishing for the millionth time that I had a mum. Even if she lived in another country, and even if she couldn't afford to send me special presents like Chelsea's mum, it would be better than no mum at all. I used to think things were perfect with just me and Dad, but it's starting to feel more and more like there's a big hole in my life that no amount of rescued spiders, mice and baby birds can fill. Dad's doing his best, but now that he's got a job he's been out all day for the last three weeks, and I've had to spend the whole time at Ed's looking after the gremlins. It's been a total nightmare.

In my dreams, my life is completely different.

If I close my eyes, I can see our home. It's not a B&B or a hostel. It's not even the one me and Dad used to rent on Ash Lane. It's a really posh house by the park, with roses round the door and a fishpond. When I come home from school, my mum greets me with a big hug and makes me a sandwich while I play with my pet dog, Bingo. I eat my snack sitting on the swings on the back lawn, then I go and do my homework in my treehouse shaped like a castle, and it's really easy cos I have a fancy phone I can use to look up all the answers on the Internet. When Dad comes home from his nice office job where he earns loads of money, we have dinner at the polished table in the dining room, just like the one I saw in Adam's house. Mum makes spaghetti bolognese cos it's my favourite, and the sauce has got proper mince and tomatoes in it instead of the dried stuff from a packet you mix with boiling water. After dinner we all watch TV together or maybe we play a game, but whatever we do it's fun and it's quiet, cos there's no one else in the giant house except us. Mum tucks me up in bed at night and Dad reads me a story, and I go to sleep thinking of all the things I'm going to do with my friends tomorrow. Maybe we'll go out for a ride on our bikes. I've got a great bike. It's a purple one with silver stripes, and—

"Norah, you missed one."

I open my eyes to see the Year Six teacher standing over me. The other kids at the table are smirking, and Chelsea's got a big grin on her face.

"Would you like me to help her, Mr Simmond? I've finished mine."

"That's kind of you, thanks Chelsea. Don't tell her the answer, though. See if you can help Norah work it out for herself."

Chelsea plonks herself down next to me and says in a big fake whisper the other kids can hear, "I know this worksheet's really tough for you cos you don't know how to spell, but if you try hard you can colour in the little pictures all by yourself. Take a good look. What else starts with the letter 'b'?"

My cheeks are burning, and my head's hanging so low it's practically buried in the worksheet. I know exactly which picture I haven't coloured in. I was avoiding it cos even looking at it makes me want to cry. Chelsea keeps pointing to it when the teacher's back is turned, and the more the tears sting my eyes, the wider her grin gets. Finally, I just give in and colour the stupid picture so she'll leave me alone, scribbling over it like the kids in nursery who don't know how to stay in the lines.

"That's right!" Chelsea says, raising her voice so everyone can hear. "'Bicycle' begins with the letter 'b'! Have *you* got a bicycle, Norah?"

The kids at the other tables turn to look. They don't know about what happened at the park in the holidays, but they can tell that something interesting's going down at our table. My face is so hot it feels like I could fry an egg on it, and I stare at the clock, willing the home-time bell to ring even though there's another twenty minutes to go. The teacher's in the store cupboard searching for another pack of whiteboard markers, and there's no one who can save me from Chelsea and her evil grin.

"I said, have *you* got a bicycle, Norah-no-mates?" she repeats, poking me in the ribs to make me answer.

I shake my head, keeping my eyes fixed on my worksheet. Jenna and Yasmin are sniggering at me across the table, and the mainstream kids are staring, and it feels like I'm up on stage with a giant spotlight shining on me.

"Oh, that's a shame," Chelsea says, making Jenna and Yasmin laugh harder. They're clearly in on the joke. "I've got a really nice bike. My brothers got it for me in the holidays. It's purple and it's got silver stripes, and there's a box on wheels attached to the back. It's a bit small for me, though, so I might give it to my little sister. She'll probably wreck it as she's just a kid and can't look after things properly, but that doesn't matter. Is that what you think I should do with the bike, Norah-no-mates? Give it to my little sister to wreck?"

You don't have a little sister! I want to tell her. *And you don't have any brothers either. They're just kids living at the foster home like you. It's not even your bike, it's mine, and if you break it I'll break your stupid head.* I don't say any of that, though. I just shrug like I don't care. Chelsea knows I care, cos no matter how hard I fight it, I can't stop the big tear that trickles down my cheek.

Before Chelsea can say anything else, the teacher comes back out and writes down the homework for the mainstream kids on the board. Chelsea goes back to her seat and whispers with her gang, and I stuff my pens and books in my schoolbag even though the bell hasn't gone. I just want to get away from Chelsea and her mean face and her lies as fast as I can.

She's not the only liar in this class, though.

I wish I could've told the truth about what happened that day. I wish I could've told Adam's mum that Chelsea and her foster brothers stole my bike, and I wish I could've let her call the police. But then they might've asked Dad lots of questions about why I was on my own, about why we were living with Ed, about whether there was enough food in the cupboards for all of us. And then they might've called social services cos they thought Dad wasn't looking after me, and I might've ended up in a foster home far apart from Dad. I might've even ended up living in Chelsea's foster home. That would be my worst nightmare.

Adam's mum didn't know I was lying, but I think Dad suspected it. He wanted to believe it was just kids I knew mucking about, though. He wanted to believe that I'd lent them my bike like I said, and that me hurting my hand and Adam falling in the pond were just accidents. He wanted it to be true cos then it would mean he wouldn't have to do anything about it. He's already got so much to deal with I'm scared one more problem might break him into little pieces.

Adam knew I was lying. I saw the way he looked at me like I was the worst person in the whole world. He'll never trust me again after I told his mum he tripped and fell into the pond when we were playing with the other kids, and he'll never want to see me again. Chelsea's right. I'm Norah-no-mates. I don't deserve any friends.

When the bell goes I take off like a rocket, running out the door and across the playground like my backside's on fire. Sometimes Chelsea's foster brothers come to pick her up from school, and I don't want to be hanging around here if they do. I push through the groups of parents crowding round the gate and hurry past all the parked cars. I'm just about to turn onto the main road when I get the funny feeling I'm being watched. I whirl round, but Chelsea and her gang aren't following me. They probably haven't even finishing packing up their schoolbags or admiring all of Chelsea's fancy presents yet.

I can't shake the weird feeling, though. I look across the road, studying the cars parked on the other side, and that's when I see it. There's a red car sitting there with the window rolled down. It's not the car I recognise, but the woman sitting in the driver's seat. She's got black hair a bit like mine, and now that she's not scowling, I can see that she really is quite pretty. She's not playing on her phone or listening to the radio like the other parents do while they're waiting for their kids to get out of school. That's probably because she isn't one of the parents.

It's the woman from the library, and she's staring right at me.

For a second I'm like a rabbit caught in the headlights, and then I turn and run even faster than before. Round the corner, up the road, across the bridge and down some back streets that bring me out to the rows of shops by the big supermarket. She won't find me now, but knowing that doesn't stop my heart from hammering in fear.

Sandra Gibson. Rainbow Children's Centre, Grimsby.

It's almost like those words have been tattooed on the inside of my eyelids and I can see them every time I close my eyes. Sandra Gibson's watching me just like a private detective, and she's trying to gather evidence that I'm not being looked after properly so she can put me in her Rainbow Children's Centre across the river where I'll never see Dad again.

I wish Dad had picked me up from school, then she'd know he really is taking care of me, I think. But Dad can't pick me up because he's working all day, and I have to go to the library till closing time to do my homework. Well, I don't *have* to exactly, but it's either that or spend the rest of the afternoon looking after Ed's screaming kids, arguing with Cheryl about using a tiny splash of milk in my cornflakes for dinner when Danny and Kayla need it for tomorrow's breakfast, and having to explain to my teacher that I couldn't do my homework yet again cos I'm living in a madhouse. If Sandra Gibson knew all that, I'd be taken away to the Rainbow Children's Centre faster than I could blink.

If I had a mum, then I wouldn't have to walk to the library all by myself, I think before I can stop myself. *She'd have been in the park looking after me while Dad was at work, and I wouldn't have had my bike stolen.*

I bite my lip. That's not fair. Dad's doing his best, and it's not his fault getting a decent job is hard and we've been homeless for ages.

But it is his fault he's lying to me about having a mother.

I don't need a mother! I'm happy with just me and Dad.

If you believe that, you wouldn't be daydreaming about a fancy house and a mum who picked you up from school and made you snacks and cooked your favourite food for dinner.

Shut up!

I kick a stone across the pavement and it clatters against the door of a charity shop. It's the one where Dad bought my school uniform last autumn, and even though I'm small, the arms of my jumper are too short and my shirt collar's too tight. I'll have to wear them till the summer holidays, though, as otherwise there'll be no money to buy my uniform for secondary school. I don't even want to think about how badly I'm going to get bullied wearing a second-hand uniform there on my first day.

There's matching boy's and girl's uniforms in the window, along with a wedding dress and a three-piece suit. But they're not what catches my eye. I'm not even interested in the board game that looks brand new or the pile of DVDs for only two pounds fifty. It's the plastic thing all scrunched up in the corner that makes me stop and peer through the glass.

I know it's a boat, as there's a little card next to it that says "Boat - £5". There's another word that starts with "i", but I give up trying to read it and just guess that it's "inflatable", cos I can see the hole at the side where you're supposed to blow it up.

I don't know why, but suddenly I want that inflatable boat more than anything.

Maybe it's cos the Year Four teacher once read us a story about a girl who floated away on a raft that took her to a magical land where wishes came true.

Maybe it's cos Dad took me to the inflatables session at the local swimming pool one birthday back when we were renting in Ash Lane, and even though I can't swim, bobbing up and down in the shallow end on a giant blow-up pirate boat was the most fun I'd ever had.

Maybe it's cos I don't have a bike anymore and Dad'll never be able to afford another one, and even though we're a million miles from the sea, I can't help dreaming about sailing away to an island where there's no homeless hostels, no social services, and no Chelsea Mackay. Me and Dad could build a house out of tree trunks and catch fish, and Bingo and me could play on the beach and build sandcastles all day. Maybe Adam would even come if I told him how sorry I was for lying to him. Maybe offering him a way to escape from his crazy-strict parents would make up for being a terrible friend.

There's a soft pattering against the window, and I look up to see dark clouds overhead again. It's been raining ever since that day in the park when I lost my bike, and my dad told me to stay away from Adam and his mum who looked down her nose at us. Rescuing animals in the park with Adam was the best thing I've done in years, and now that's over it's like all the sunshine has gone out of my life and no amount of banana milkshake will ever be able to bring it back.

There's no point thinking about that now. I need to stop standing here daydreaming, or I'm going to spend the rest of the afternoon in soaking wet clothes.

I pull up the hood of the jacket that's too small for me, and trudge through the puddles in my scuffed shoes all the way to the library on the other side of town.

Chapter 14

ADAM

It's the same dream every night. I'm in the Aquatic Centre in Leeds, lined up in the pool with the nine other kids and we're about to race for the regional under tens' 200m trophy. I'm going to win this race. I know I will, as it's already happened and the trophy's sitting on my bookshelf at home. The stands are packed with parents, and even some of my teachers and school friends have come to see me race. The lights are so bright they're almost blinding, but I can see my mother and father waving to me from the front row.

I don't have time to wave back, though, as the whistle goes and I launch myself through the water. I'm like one of those speed boats I saw on holiday in Spain before I was sick, cutting through the blue water at a hundred miles per hour and capsizing jet skiers and wind surfers in the powerful waves it sent up. I'm unstoppable, leaving behind all the other swimmers who are too slow to catch me. I touch the opposite wall, turn, and start tearing back down my lane. I'm going to win this! I'm going to win—

But then suddenly the lights go out.

The whole pool is plunged into darkness, and the water turns thick and sticky like I'm trying to swim through treacle. I start to sink, flailing about and yelling for help. Only there's no one here. All of the other kids in the pool have disappeared, and the spectators' stands are empty.

No, I'm wrong—there are two people still watching me. My mother and father are standing at the side of the pool, and they're crying and wringing their hands, but they're not trying to pull me out. My arms and legs feel weak, and I don't have the energy to fight the water that's dragging me under the surface.

"Help me!" I yell, reaching out for my parents. Their eyes are wide with worry and I've never seen them looking so scared before, but it's like they're frozen, and they don't know what to do. "Adam!" they call back helplessly. "Adam!"

The water closes over my head and rushes down my throat, and I know I'm going to drown. Underwater, everything's muffled, but I can hear my heart hammering in my chest, the sound of my lungs choking, and the faraway cry of my parents calling my name.

"Adam!"

The voice isn't far away, it's right next to my ear.

I jerk awake, sitting bolt upright and staring round my room in confusion. It's broad daylight, and my father's pulling back the curtains.

"Adam, it's four in the afternoon. It's not good for you to stay in bed sleeping all day."

I rub my eyes, trying to get rid of the dream that's been haunting me ever since that boy pushed me into the duck pond. My father doesn't sit on my bed and offer to tell me a story or watch a film with me like he's done for the last few weeks. Instead, he gets some clothes out of my drawers and pulls the covers off my bed.

"Come on, you need to get up. I'm putting the barbecue on."

We haven't had a barbecue in ages. A few weeks ago I would've killed to have my father take time away from his computer to cook us some burgers, but now I just clutch at my quilt and try to draw it back over my head. "I'm not feeling well enough," I say weakly. "I'll just stay here. Maybe you could bring me a burger when it's done?"

"You're not staying in bed. You're getting up."

There's a new note in my father's voice, and it's not one I like.

"But I'm not feeling well!" I whine.

"*Adam.*" My father finally sits on my bed, but the look on his face is stern. "We've taken you to the hospital three times. They've run every test they have. There's nothing wrong with you that a bit of fresh air and exercise won't fix. So stop this nonsense and get yourself dressed. I need you to come and help me cook those burgers."

He marches downstairs before I can protest again. I get out of bed slowly and take my time pulling on my clothes, making it look like way more effort than it is even though no one's watching me. As far as I'm concerned I'm sick and fragile and I might just break if I make too much effort to do anything. Isn't that what my mother's been telling me for months? Isn't this what she wanted—me wrapped up safe in bed where she can keep a permanent eye on me?

I drag my feet walking down the stairs, clomping on each step as though moving is painful, just like it was when I had cancer. My mother's in the kitchen baking another of my favourite cakes, and she looks up in surprise when I trudge in.

"Adam! What are you doing out of bed?"

"Dad says I have to help with the barbecue," I mutter.

"Don't be ridiculous! You'll catch your death of cold out there. Go right back up to bed and I'll bring you—"

"It hasn't rained all day!" My father puts his head back round the door and frowns at my mother. "He needs to get a bit of fresh air. Come on, Adam, you can help me heat the coals."

"But it's freezing out there!" my mother protests. "Adam isn't well, he's—"

"Helen, we've talked about this." His voice is quiet, but so stern my mother shuts her mouth and glares at the door when he goes back out.

"Make sure you wrap up warmly with your winter coat," she says to me, even less happy about the barbecue than I am. "And come straight back in if you're feeling cold, OK?"

I frown at her so she knows I'm not happy that she's siding with my father, and go and fetch my winter coat and scarf. I used to wear a hat even in warmer weather when I lost my hair as my head got so cold, but I think that might be overdoing it now, and I leave it in the coat cupboard.

My father gives me an encouraging smile when I sit down on the garden bench, but I shake my head when he offers to let me stir up the barbecue coals. I'm too ill to do any work. I don't know why he isn't being nice to me today.

The last few weeks have been great. My father switched to working from home, and he's been spending almost as much time with me as he did when I had cancer. We've been playing board games on my bed as a whole family and eating dinner together every night. Going to the hospital so I could be tested was almost like going on a proper family outing. I don't know why my father's saying I'm well again and trying to ruin everything. If he doesn't believe me, he might go back to work, and then I won't get to spend any more time with him. I have to make him see I really am sick.

I start coughing hard even though my throat doesn't tickle, and that has my mother running out with a glass of water and a blanket to wrap me in. My father frowns and shakes his head, and she scowls back and checks my forehead to make sure I don't have a fever.

"Adam, come and help me put the burgers on," my father says, like he's trying to get me away from her.

"It's better if he goes back inside," my mother snaps, "he's not—"

"He's *fine*."

My mother's glare is even hotter than the glowing barbecue coals, and she stomps back into the kitchen angrily. There's something going on with my parents, and although I'm at the centre of it like I wanted, this isn't the way it's supposed to be. I grab the spatula my father holds out to me and dump the burgers onto the barbecue without any enthusiasm. They start sizzling, and we add some sausages and sweetcorn. My father encourages me to help him make up some vegetable kebabs, and soon I forget I'm supposed to be sick and just enjoy being out with him in the garden.

I shouldn't have let my guard down, though, as the next thing he asks me knocks me sideways.

"So, I've been thinking," he says. "Your tutor says you're ready to go back to school, and your doctors think so too. It would be good to finish the last term at the local school so you can make some friends there before secondary school. That way, you can all move up to Year Seven together. What do you think?"

"Um…" I don't know what to think. A few weeks ago, I was desperate to go to school. But when my father thought I was better, he just stayed at work all day and sat in his study at weekends and ignored me. Since he thought I was sick again he's been spending all his time with me. It feels like he's asking me to choose between having a normal life like I wanted but not getting to see him, and pretending to be ill and spending lots of time with him.

How am I supposed to make a choice like that?

Fortunately I don't have to, as my mother heard what he said and comes running out like the house is on fire.

"What are you *thinking*, Fraser?" she snaps. "You know Adam's not well enough to even be considering school right now."

"There's nothing wrong with him!" My father throws a kebab skewer down on the tray. "But if you keep babying him, he's never going to get back to school!"

"He's doing well with his tutor. Aren't you, Adam?"

Both my parents turn to me, and I feel like I'm the judge on the TV show that my mother doesn't like me watching because she thinks it's "trashy". Except that judge always seems to know the right decision to make, and I haven't a clue. Whatever I say, I'm going to disappoint one of them.

"Um…" I say again. It's not very helpful, but at least it makes my father see I probably shouldn't be stuck in the middle of this.

"Helen, come back into the house. I want to talk to you for a minute."

"We've talked about this till we're blue in the face, Fraser!"

"And we clearly need to discuss it some more!"

They go back inside, still glaring daggers at each other, and I can hear their angry voices carrying through the kitchen. I can't make out what they're saying, but I know it's all about me and whether I really am sick or not. I heave a big sigh, then I stick a burger in one of the buttered buns and sit down on the bench to eat it. There's no point in me trying to lose weight now. I'm never going to be an Olympic swimmer, and after that awful day in the pond, I don't ever want to be in a swimming pool again.

There's no point in me making decisions about whatever I want, either. I've learned over the last six months that it doesn't matter—my parents are just going to decide what's best for me and no amount of pleading or arguing is going to change their minds. I wish they could agree, though—hearing them argue like this is making me feel so bad I can hardly swallow my burger.

It's starting to rain, so I pull up my hood and transfer all of the cooked food to the covered dish my father's left out to keep it warm. I'm just about to carry it back inside when I hear another sound that isn't my parents arguing in the kitchen. It's a harsh mewling—half angry, half begging. I look down and see the ginger cat watching me from under the hedge. Her fur is matted and her collar's scuffed, and the metal nametag that says "Marmalade" on it looks like it needs a good polish.

I always thought I hated cats, but there's something about the way she's crying and sniffing the air like the smell of food's driving her mad that makes me feel really sorry for her. I take a sausage out of the dish and kneel down, holding it out to her. Her ears prick up, but she's nervous, creeping forward slowly like she doesn't trust me. I put it down on the ground and shuffle back, and she darts out and grabs the sausage before running back under the hedge again. She keeps her eyes on me the whole time she's eating it, her green eyes studying my face like she's trying to work out if I'm just pretending to be nice so I can hurt her.

Then she does something really weird.

Instead of running off when she's finished, she comes creeping back out again and rubs herself against my leg. I'm not sure what to do, so I bend down and scratch her under the chin. She seems to like that, as she starts purring. "So, you don't hate me after all, do you, Marmalade?" I grin.

She looks up at me through narrowed eyes and meows again, and I'm pretty sure she's just being friendly because she wants me to give her more food. I know why she's even hungrier than usual. Her belly's swollen like a pink balloon, and when it pops there's going to be even more ginger cats prowling about our garden trying to steal the last of my father's goldfish.

The rain's coming down harder now, and it shows just how bad my parents' argument is, because my mother hasn't even noticed and come rushing out to tell me to get inside. The cat's going to get soaked again, and she's already in pretty bad shape. I hesitate for a minute as an idea starts to form in my head. I don't want to get into trouble for feeding Marmalade and encouraging her to come begging in the garden, especially as it'll remind my mother that she was going to call the local animal home about her. But I don't want her being cold and wet and hungry out here with nowhere for her and her kittens to go either. And that leaves only one option.

I take a burger and another sausage from the dish and hold them out to the cat, but when she comes to get them, I move away. She follows me, and I move up the grass again. She gets frustrated and hisses at me when we're halfway to the big tree at the bottom of the garden, but I give her a bit of the burger to show her I'm not just teasing her, and she follows me all the way up the ladder to the treehouse after that.

"There you go." I put the food down on the floor and Marmalade snaffles it up in case I change my mind again. Then she stretches herself, gives a big yawn and jumps up onto my comfy chair to snuggle into the blanket. She's been here less than two minutes and already it looks like she owns the place.

"That's it, I'm not calling you 'Marmalade' anymore!" I laugh. "It's a stupid name, anyway. I'm calling you 'Lady' since you act like royalty. You'd better come when I call you, though, because I'm not your servant and I might not bring you any more food unless you're nice to me."

Lady knows it's an empty threat. She already has me wrapped around her little finger, or little paw, or whatever it is that cats wrap stupid humans around. She yawns again like she's dismissing me, then she settles down to go to sleep. I leave her to it. She might just bite my hand off if I try to pat her now. I carry a couple of big stones up the ladder and wedge the treehouse open just a crack so the cat can get in and out, but so it won't bang back and forth in the wind. I don't want my mother knowing there's anything going on up here that she wouldn't like.

If I don't get back inside before I'm soaked, that might make my parents argue even more. I don't think my father's worried about me drowning in a bit of rain like my mother is, and her fussing seems to annoy him even more than it used to annoy me. I hurry back to the house, trying to forget that I've been feeling totally fine for the last hour and trying to remind myself I'm ill. If I don't, then I know I'll be disappointed when my mother wins the argument with my father and sends me back to bed again. It felt so good when Norah was my friend and I had a bit of freedom with her, and then so awful when my mother said I couldn't see her again. I never want to have my hope crushed like that ever again.

Better just to let my mother have her own way and do what I'm told, even if it makes me feel cold and grey inside just like the sky above our house.

Chapter 15

NORAH

It's four o'clock on a Saturday afternoon, and Ed's house is the most chaotic it's ever been. Dad hasn't had more than a couple of hours at the warehouse all week, and he's in the kitchen having a big argument with Ed over the fact that there's no food in the fridge yet again. Cheryl's in one of the bedrooms yelling at her brother cos he got caught by the police selling packets of stolen cigarettes, and now he has to go to court. That leaves me to look after all five gremlins by myself.

Mikie's having a hard time with sore gums now that his teeth are coming in, so none of us have had any proper sleep for days. Kayla's howling cos Toby ate her bag of crisps and she hasn't eaten since breakfast. Chris and Toby are knocking lumps out of each other, and their flailing arms and legs have already broken the lamp next to the TV. Danny's screaming at the top of his lungs cos I told him five times not to swing from the curtains, but he went and did it anyway and landed headfirst on the floorboards when they tore.

I'm shouting at Chris and Toby, trying to coax Kayla to eat a day-old slice of toast instead, jiggling Mikie up and down on my shoulder to stop him crying, and trying to stick a plaster over the cut on Danny's forehead with my free hand.

And that's when social services knock on the door.

I open it cos I think it's one of Ed's mates, and maybe they're bringing money that they won on the fruit machines and we might be able to buy takeout tonight. But it's not. It's two women in smart clothes with nice accents who ask if Dad's home. If my head wasn't so muddled through lack of sleep, I might be able to think of an excuse fast enough, but my brain's mush and I just gawp at them with my mouth open. They size up the baby in my left arm, the toddler with the broken head hanging off the other, and gaze past me into the madhouse beyond.

Then they exchange glances.

That's when I know me and Dad are in a lot of trouble. I go running into the kitchen, calling for him to come *right now* and talk to the women at the door. When they introduce themselves as Linda and Kathy from the social work department, his face goes white and he looks look he's going to pass out. The gremlins go quiet too, and Ed has no trouble for once packing them off to the big bedroom to keep them out of the way.

"Norah, go and check on the kids. I need to talk to these ladies," Dad says, trying to pretend everything's alright even though I can see it's not.

"I'll just fix Mikie a bottle first," I say, taking him to the kitchen where it's easier to hear what the women are saying to Ed and Dad. At first there's just hushed voices through the door, then one woman says a bit louder, "Didn't you get the letter from the housing office, Mr Prichard? There's been a complaint about over occupancy— there's too many people living here."

"Letter?" I can hear Ed rifling through the pile of mail by the TV. He just throws everything that comes through the door there where it builds up into an unopened mountain of paper. "Oh, right. This." I hear him tearing the envelope open. "I thought it was just another bill."

"Well, they gave you a week to sort the situation out. That was a week ago. If it's not fixed by five pm today, then the housing office will have to also evict you and your family for non-compliance."

I don't know what all the big words mean, but I'm pretty good at guessing. Someone's complained about all the people in the council flat, and me and Dad have to leave tonight or Ed's family will get kicked out too. It's so unfair! If we had anywhere else to go we wouldn't be living in this madhouse, would we? And what if we can't find somewhere else in the next hour? Are they going to take me away from Dad and stick me in a foster home?

Mikie can feel my chest heaving in fear, and he starts whimpering again. I shush him and press my ear against the door, trying to hear what the grown-ups in the living room are saying. I can hear Dad clearly enough. He's trying to stay calm, but he's close to breaking point, and his voice is getting louder and louder.

"How the hell can the housing office kick me out of here when they know I've got nowhere to go? You think I want to drag my daughter from place to place for the fun of it? I wouldn't be in this mess if the government could just get my benefits right! They've messed my payments up three times in the last year because I've been in and out of work, and each time my daughter and I have got evicted because of unpaid rent. Now you're telling me I can't even keep a roof over her head by staying with a friend? What the hell do you want us to do? Go and live on the street? Yeah, you'd love that, wouldn't you, cos then you could say I'm an unfit parent and take my daughter off me! You're not taking Norah, d'you hear me? You're not—"

I can't help gasping in shock. Dad's doing something I've never heard him do before.

He's crying.

I forget all about Mikie's milk and go running back into the living room. I practically throw Mikie at Ed and run to hug Dad. "They're not taking me away, are they? You said you wouldn't let them! You said—"

Before I know it, I'm crying too and holding onto Dad so tight my fingers hurt. He's got his head in his hands and his shoulders are heaving, and his big ugly sobs are making his whole body shake. That scares me even more. I always thought Dad could protect me from anything, and seeing him so helpless is the most frightening thing that's ever happened to me.

Ed takes Mikie away and goes to talk to Cheryl before she can come barging in to find out what's happening. The women start talking again, but it takes me and Dad some time to calm down enough to hear what they're saying.

"We're not here to take Norah into care," the one called Linda says soothingly. "That's not what this is about. We're here to help. There's been an anonymous complaint made about your situation with your daughter, but before we deal with that, we need to sort out the housing situation, OK?"

Dad nods, trying to get his breathing under control again. Kathy comes back from the kitchen with a glass of water for him, and he drinks it with a shaking hand. He keeps his arms wrapped tightly round me as they talk, like he believes they'll whisk me away if he lets go. They go through the benefits payments that Dad's missed out on due to the mistakes the government department keeps making, the lost money from job centre sanctions for things that weren't his fault, the evictions for not paying rent when we weren't given the money to pay, and all the other things that have been making our lives a misery. I can recite the whole lot off the top of my head by now, I've heard Dad tell the job centre so many times.

Linda's writing it all down and frowning. "Right, there's definitely grounds for making a claim for all the lost benefits. Have you—"

"I've filled in the forms with the job centre three times now, and sat on the phone for hours, but nothing's ever come of it," Dad sighs, sounding defeated.

"Well, we'll help you with it. In the meantime, I'll make some calls to see if we can get you and Norah somewhere temporary."

Kathy goes to the kitchen to make some calls, and I snuggle into Dad's chest and tune out the conversation he has with Linda about his job and if he's managing to save money. It's bad enough he lies to me, I don't want to hear him lying to anyone else about trying to save money. We're not just broke because the benefit payments are always wrong and he only gets jobs with rubbish pay and zero-hour contracts. I know he goes to the betting shop with Ed. I know we're in this rubbish situation because he must be spending our money on the horses and the fruit machines just like he blames Ed for doing, or else why would he go there?

I just wish he loved me enough to admit the truth for once.

"We've found you a place at a hostel not far from here that'll take you both for two weeks," Kathy says when she comes back in. "Norah, why don't you start packing your things and we'll drive you over when you're ready?"

I'm not an idiot. I know that means they're sending me out of the room so they can talk to Dad about the other thing—the thing they said about someone making an anonymous complaint about him not looking after me properly. I grab my schoolbag and go to the big bedroom where the four oldest gremlins are sitting on the beds quiet as mice. Their eyes are wide, and they watch me with open mouths as I shove the clothes scattered on the floor into my bag. Poor kids. They're terrified it's them social services have come for. Knowing Ed and Cheryl, it probably wouldn't be the first time.

Most of our stuff hasn't been unpacked cos there was nowhere to put it, so I pull our suitcases out of the cupboard in the hall. While the adults are still talking and the gremlins are out of the way, I open them up and do a quick check to make sure Ed and Jim haven't nicked anything. I wouldn't put it past them.

We don't have much that's worth anything anymore, as it all got pawned off and sold over the last couple of years. The stuff that's left is mostly things like the album of my baby photos, Dad's football medals from school, and folders full of evidence for the job centre to show them he's been looking for work. There's one shoebox at the bottom of Dad's big suitcase that I haven't opened before. I saw him looking through it once in one of the hostels we lived in, and when I asked, he said it was just some old newspaper clippings from when he played in football matches with his school team. He put them away pretty quick instead of showing them to me, but I didn't think anything of it at the time.

Now, after all the lies, everything Dad does makes me suspicious.

I glance round to make sure everyone's still busy, then I open the shoebox to see what's inside. At first I'm disappointed. It is just newspaper stories about football matches after all. I'm about to put the box back when I notice there's a small bundle of photos underneath the clippings. I pull them out, flicking through them. They're of Dad when he was younger. He's got a beard, which is really funny, and a bad haircut that makes him look like he's been drowned in a bucket of gel. He's sitting on a motorbike trying to look cool, but he's laughing too hard to pull it off. That's the nice thing about the photos—how happy he looks. He's grinning at the person taking the pictures like the whole world is full of cupcakes and unicorns and banana-milkshake sunshine. I haven't seen him smile like that in years.

I've only got a couple of photos left to look at, when Dad calls from the living room, "Is that you sorted, Norah?"

"Just coming!" I call back, glancing at one of the last photos before I drop them into the box with the rest. My eyes nearly pop out of my head when I see it. It isn't a picture of Dad. It's a picture of a pretty young woman sitting on Dad's motorbike and smiling at the camera. She's got black hair like mine, and brown eyes just like me instead of Dad's blue ones. She looks a lot younger in the picture, but I can still recognise her. She's the woman from the library. The woman who was watching me from her car after school. The familiar words flash through my head again before I can stop them.

Sandra Gibson. Rainbow Children's Centre, Grimsby.

Is the social worker who's trying to get me taken into care actually Dad's old *girlfriend*?

Before I can work it out, Dad brings his rucksack out and dumps it in the hall beside the suitcases I've already wheeled out of the cupboard. I close the box quickly, shoving the last of the pictures in my pocket before he can see them, then I zip the case and grab my jacket. The next few minutes are a blur of goodbyes and hugs, and you'd think the gremlins actually liked me the way they hang onto me and beg me not to go. I thought I'd be relieved to get away from Ed's madhouse, but moving to new places is always stressful. By the time I'm sitting in Linda's car and she starts the engine, my insides are a big knot of nerves.

I hoped the hostel would be far away from Ed's house and the betting shop so Dad wouldn't be able to see him there much, but it's only a ten-minute walk away. When we get there, Linda and Dad get out to speak to the hostel manager first, and I sit in the car with Kathy till they come back.

Kathy tries to ask me questions about school and if I'm happy there, but there's only one thing I want to talk to her about. I take a deep breath and say, "Do you work with a woman called Sandra Gibson? Is she a social worker at your office?"

Kathy looks a bit surprised and shakes her head. "There's no one at the office called Sandra. I should know, I've been there ten years."

"Oh. I thought she was the one who wanted to take me into foster care, you know, to the Rainbow Children's Centre?"

"The Rainbow Centre in Grimsby? Social services wouldn't take you there, pet, that's a private nursery school, not a foster home."

"Oh," I say again. Now I'm more confused than ever.

Kathy thinks it's because I'm still scared of being taken away from Dad, and says quickly, "Don't worry about foster care, Norah. I know it sounds frightening, but it's the last thing we do, and only if everything else doesn't work. You and your dad have somewhere to stay for the next few weeks, and Linda and I will be popping over to check how you're getting on and lending a hand if there's anything you need. We're here to help you both, OK?"

That makes me a feel a bit better. I'm not going to end up living with Chelsea Mackay and her foster brothers for a couple of weeks, at least. When Dad and Linda come back out, we unload our suitcases and bags and carry them inside. It's a big building that only has two floors, so there's lots of corridors to go down to find our room, and I start to wonder if I'm going to get lost and never find my way back out. The room's not bad, though. It doesn't have a TV or a kettle, but it does have its own small bathroom. Even though the shower drips, at least that means it actually works, not like some of the places we've been in.

Linda and Kathy are really nice, but I'm desperate for them to leave to give me a chance to look at the photos that feel like they're on fire inside my pocket. When Dad goes out into the corridor with them to say goodbye and thank them for their help, I run to the bathroom, locking the door behind me and whipping the pictures out. The second one's of the same woman, only this time she's standing in a garden with a flowery dress on, her hands around her belly. She looks pregnant.

I nearly drop the last picture on the floor.

The woman's sitting up in a hospital bed, holding a baby. Dad's got his arms round her, and they're both smiling down at the baby instead of looking at the camera. When I turn the picture over there's writing on the back, and when I concentrate really hard I finally work out that the words say "Baby Norah, and the world's happiest mum and dad!" My head starts to pound and the knot in my stomach grows so big I can barely breathe. Now I finally know what Dad's been lying to me about.

The woman who's been following me isn't from social services.

She's my mum.

Chapter 16

ADAM

It's the same dream, over and over again. I'm drowning in the pool; my parents are standing watching me, but no one's trying to save me.

This time it's the rain pounding against the window that wakes me. I probably should've been up hours ago. It's eleven o'clock on a Sunday morning, and I've been in bed for ages. I don't want to get up yet, though. My mother's at church, and as usual my father's spending his Sunday morning in his study working. If I get up now, he might think I really am better, and then I won't be able to guilt-trip him into watching films with me after lunch. I have to be really careful not to overdo the sick act around him now, as whenever I try to get attention by asking him to help me with something he knows I can do, he just snaps, "You're not a baby, Adam, you can do it yourself."

I'm so confused. When I had cancer, my parents spent every second they could with me, and they were desperate for me to get well so I could have a normal life again. But when I got better, my mother acted like she thought I was still sick, and my father acted like I was invisible. At first pretending to be sick seemed like it would fix things, at least with my father. But now my parents are arguing all the time about me, and I don't know whether to be sick like my mother wants or well like my father wants.

All I know is I can't win either way.

My window bangs again, and I look up to see it's swung open and is letting the rain in over my desk. I can't be bothered getting up to close it, but the books my tutor lent me for my climate change project are getting wet. It's bad enough I'm lying and saying I'm too sick to study with him—I don't want to hand back a pile of soggy books too when my mother eventually decides I'm well enough for lessons again. I pull back my quilt and go over to close the window softly so my father doesn't hear I'm up.

I'm just about to go back to bed again, when something outside catches my eye.

There's a light flickering from the treehouse at the bottom of the garden. On, off, on, off it flashes, almost like someone's up there signalling me. The rain's too heavy for me to see if there's a face at the window, but there's only one person in the world who'd be in my treehouse trying to get my attention, and it certainly isn't the cat I've hidden in there. I hesitate, torn between the urge to ignore the signal so I can go back to bed and keep playing sick, and the tingle of excitement that runs up my spine at the thought of adventure.

My father's study faces the front garden, but if he goes into the kitchen to make a cup of coffee he might see the flashing light, and if my mother heard about who he'd find in the treehouse, then I wouldn't be the only one in trouble. That's what makes up my mind for me.

I throw a pair of jeans and a jumper on over my pyjamas, and tiptoe down the stairs so my father won't hear me. My rubber boots are in the cupboard by the back door, and I take the big golf umbrella too, so I won't get wet. Before I sneak out, I pull the tray of last night's barbecue leftovers from the fridge and dump half of the sausages and burgers into a plastic bag. I know it won't just be Lady who's hungry up there.

I close the back door behind me as softly as I can and race for the big tree at the bottom of the garden, my boots squelching on the grass. The fishpond's overflowing, and there's a giant puddle by the fence that's drowned my mother's favourite flowers. If this rain doesn't stop soon, my mother's going to be swimming home from church instead of driving.

The steps on the treehouse ladder are slippery and it's not easy climbing up one-handed, trying to hold the golf umbrella with the other. I put my head round the door that I've propped open with stones, but what I see inside isn't exactly what I'm expecting. Norah's just as wet as I thought she'd be, but Lady isn't hissing at her or trying to claw her hands to shreds. She's curled up in the blanket on Norah's lap, purring like she's in cat heaven as Norah scratches her ears. Even if Norah can't be a vet when she's older, she's certainly got a way with animals.

"Norah! What are you doing in here?"

She puts down the bike headlight that she's been using as a signal, and looks at me warily like she's not sure if I'll be nice to her or not. She looks a bit like Lady did yesterday under the hedge, all bedraggled and suspicious but desperate for me not to chase her away.

"I'm sorry," she says, "but I didn't know who else I could talk to. I know your mum said I'm not supposed to see you again, and I know you probably don't want to see me anyway, but..." She trails off, waiting to see if I'm still mad at her for what happened at the pond. I was until about ten seconds ago. Now seeing her here, I'm just glad I haven't lost the only friend I've had in ages.

"How come you lied, Norah?" I ask, sitting down in the other chair and trying not to be jealous that Lady's snuggling up with Norah and ignoring me. "How come you said those kids who took your bike were your friends and I fell in the pond by accident? You made me look like a liar!"

Norah stares at the ground, water dripping from her tangled hair onto the floor. "I was scared," she says softly.

"Of getting into trouble? No one would've blamed you. It wasn't your fault."

"Yeah, but—" Norah bites her lip and takes a deep breath. "If your mum had called the police, then they might've called social services. I was scared we'd get investigated, and they'd find out how long we've been homeless for, and that there wasn't much food in the house we were staying in."

I blink at her. I'm so stupid. After everything she's told me, I should've worked out that things were difficult enough for her at home without having to deal with a police investigation.

"It doesn't matter now," she shrugs, "cos they came yesterday anyway."

"What did they do?" For a second my heart's in my mouth as I think Norah's run away, and I'm going to have to hide her in my treehouse along with the cat that's about to have kittens.

"They were actually really nice," she says. "They found us somewhere else to stay, and they're helping my dad sort out all the problems with his benefits cos the stupid government office keeps getting them wrong."

"But that's good, isn't it? Norah, how come you look sad?"

Norah's face crumples, and she starts crying. Lady decides she doesn't like getting rained on, and comes over to sit in my lap instead. "Dad's lying to me!" Norah sniffs. "Not like he used to, about little things that aren't important, but about big things!"

"Like what?" I feel kind of awkward. I want to reach over and take her hand, but I don't want her to think I'm totally soppy, and anyway Lady's pawing at me, trying to get at the food in my pocket. That stupid cat could have World War Three going on around her and she wouldn't care as long as she was getting food and attention. No wonder I'm a dog person.

"He says he never gambles at the betting shop and he just goes there to watch TV, but I know he goes there all the time, and we never have any money!"

"But you said that's because the benefits office keeps getting the payments wrong."

"That what he tells me, but now I don't believe him!"

"How come?"

"Because he's lying to me about something even bigger!"

"What?" I lean forward, nearly sending Lady tumbling from my lap.

Norah gulps hard and pulls a photograph from her pocket, handing it over to me. It's of her dad and a woman sitting on a hospital bed, and they're holding a baby. I take one look at the writing on the back and understand straight away why Norah's so upset.

"He always said I didn't have a mum, but I do! I've *seen* her, Adam! She's been talking to my dad, and he keeps telling her I'm his and she can't see me, but she's been following me around. She gave Dad her number—here," she hands me a Sellotaped business card.

"The Rainbow Children's Centre is a nursery in Grimsby, across the river. I think that's where she works."

I stare at the card, then back at Norah. "Are you going to call her?"

"I don't know. Do you think I should?"

"I don't know." That's not much help, but I can't even sort out the mess of my own life, so what hope do I have of helping Norah with her problems? There's only one thing I can solve right now, and that's how hungry she and Lady both are. I take out my bag of barbecue leftovers and share them round, making sure Lady doesn't snaffle the last sausage before Norah can reach it. Once she's finished, Norah looks a bit better, and the colour's back in her pale cheeks. She gives the last bite of sausage to Lady, then throws me a sideways look.

"I thought you said you hated cats and that this ginger one was a menace."

"Yeah, but that was before I found out my neighbours moved away and abandoned her, and she's been hungry for months."

"Oh. Poor thing." Norah strokes Lady's ears gently, and now that my food's gone Lady decides she prefers Norah's lap better after all. Traitor. "So your parents let you keep her?"

"Not exactly…" I shake my head. "I think my dad wouldn't mind, but my mother will kill me if she finds Lady up here."

"Lady?" Norah looks at the cat's collar like she can't quite work out what it says, but knows there's too many letters there.

"Yeah, it's short for 'Marmalade.'"

"That's a stupid name." Norah rolls her eyes. "They might as well just've called her 'Jam' or 'Peanut Butter.'"

I try not to look surprised that Norah actually knows what marmalade is. I've made way too many wrong assumptions about her already.

"So what are you going to do when she has kittens? Are you going to keep them?"

"I don't know," I shrug again.

"But what if your mother finds out about them?"

"I don't know that either." I have no answers for anything today. I've never felt more useless in all my life.

Norah nods sadly. I think she knows exactly what it's like to feel helpless. "At least they'll be warm and dry in here," she says, "not like out there. My dad says it's the worst rain there's ever been in Hull, but I don't know if I believe him about that either."

"It's true," I tell her, before she can get upset about her dad lying to her again. "I've been doing a project about climate change, and it's definitely making the storms in the UK worse."

I point to all the charts and pictures I've printed out and stuck to the treehouse walls. Norah squints at them like they're written in a foreign language. "But I thought global warming was the world getting hotter cos there's too many cars on the road and we use too much plastic or something."

"It is. It's about us cutting down rainforests and burning coal and oil for energy and not recycling, and a million other things we're doing to wreck the planet," I tell her. "When the world gets hotter, the ice in cold places melts and the sea levels rise. The sun evaporates more water— you know, turns it into steam? And then that steam turns into rain, like we're getting way too much of just now."

"Oh." She puzzles it out. "So how do we fix it?"

Norah's finally asked me something I actually have an answer for. I grin and grab my notebook, showing her all the printouts and magazine clippings I've done for my project about how we can recycle more and cut down on the amount of coal and oil the world uses.

I'm so busy talking I don't hear the footsteps on the treehouse ladder until it's too late.

"Adam! What on earth's going on in here?"

I look up in alarm, and drop my notebook. My mother's standing at the door, her eyes wide with shock as she stares first at Norah, then at Lady.

"Um, Norah was just checking to see if I was alright," I say quickly. "Dad says I'm much better now and I can go back to school, so there's no reason I can't have friends over now, is there?"

My mother looks like I've just told her I'm an alien from a distant planet who's only pretending to be her real son. "Adam! You're far too ill to be seeing anyone, and you'll catch your death of cold out here in the rain. Norah, go home now, please, and don't come back here. You're putting Adam at risk of catching germs."

Norah doesn't argue. She just stares down at her grubby clothes and scuffed shoes like she's really ashamed. That makes me mad. "Norah's my friend!" I protest. "And I'll see her if I want!"

Instead of getting angry back, my mother gives me *that* look. The one I kept seeing in the hospital. The one from my nightmares where I'm drowning in the swimming pool. The look that's so full of fear it makes my stomach do sick somersaults and my heart pound. "Adam, *please*," she says like she's choking. "It's dangerous!"

Norah looks from me to my mother, then back at me again. She might not be any good at reading, but she's an expert at working people out. "I've got to go," she decides, grabbing her backpack and shoving her bike headlight inside.

"Tell your father I'll speak to him next time I see him in church," my mother says sternly. "In the meantime, Adam, lock the door behind you. I'm calling the animal shelter, and I don't want that stray cat escaping before they can come and collect it."

My mother marches down the ladder and back to the house before I can try to change her mind. As if I'd bother. I learned a long time ago that was a waste of my time.

Norah and I exchange worried looks. "Animal shelter?" Norah gulps. "Don't they put abandoned cats and dogs to sleep there?"

"If they're not adopted in a few weeks, then yeah," I nod. "And who's going to adopt a mangy orange cat that's about to have kittens?"

"Isn't there someone else who can take her?"

"I don't know anyone else. There's just you."

"*Me?*" Norah looks at me like I'm mad. "How am I supposed to take a cat back to the homeless shelter? I wasn't even allowed to keep Bingo, and I wanted him more than anything."

"I know!" I snap, "but there must be somewhere else you can keep her where she'll be out of the rain—a shed or an abandoned car or *something*." My throat's all tight with anger and frustration, and I can feel my eyes start to water. I'm so sick of feeling helpless, but I'm even more scared of that terrible look in my mother's eyes that says if I don't do what I'm told she'll fall apart with worry and then our whole world might end.

I glance out of the window. I can see my mother standing at the kitchen door, her mobile phone clamped to her ear. She's calling the animal shelter, and when she sees me looking out, she waves me over. "*Come here right now!*" she mouths. I'm out of time, and out of options.

"I suppose there's one place…" Norah says suddenly, making my heart leap in hope. "But—"

"It doesn't matter if it's not perfect," I say quickly before she can change her mind. "Just as long as it's dry and safe. Here, take this." I rummage in my jeans pockets and find a five-pound note and some coins that Dad gave me for pocket money the other day. "You can buy her some food so you don't get into trouble with your dad."

Norah takes the money reluctantly. I can tell she doesn't like the idea of taking my money, but it's not for her, it's for the cat, so it's not charity or anything. Before my mother can come stomping back, I help her put Lady into her backpack and zip it up. Lady doesn't like it at first and squirms about, trying to get free, but then when Norah slings it over her shoulder she settles down.

Norah stops at the top of the ladder, looking up at me sadly with rain running down her face like tears. "Adam? I can't come back to your garden. My dad won't go to church anymore in case he bumps into your mum there. He won't let me come here again, and neither will your mum. Will I see you again?"

I say the same thing I've been saying all morning, and it makes me feel so helpless it's like I'm back in the hospital again attached to machines that are doing all my body's work for me as I'm too weak.

"I don't know, Norah. I just don't know."

Chapter 17

NORAH

"What about these ones? There's a bit more room in the toe. What do you think?"

"Um…" I blink at the guy in the shoe shop, trying to concentrate on his questions, but my head's so full of the photos of my mother I can't think straight. I look to my dad for the answer instead. He's frowning at the price on the box, and that decides it. They're six pounds dearer than the first pair we looked at, and the emergency loan that Kathy at social services managed to get for us isn't going to stretch that far.

"The first pair's fine," I say without enthusiasm. They're the cheapest pair in the shop, and I bet everyone in school will know it. At least they're not from a charity shop like the "new" jacket we just picked up. I'm trying really hard to be grateful, but it's tough when I know the mean kids at school will laugh at everything Dad gets for me.

I swing my legs and drum my fingers on the chair as I wait for the guy to go and fetch the shoebox from the storeroom. I can't look Dad in the eye anymore. Ever since I found those photos, I've felt like I've been living with a total stranger. He's been lying to me for years, and he's still doing it.

"What's up, Sunny, hmm?" he asks, trying to catch my eye. "You're looking all glum. Do you like the other shoes better? We can get those ones if you want."

"These ones are fine. Thanks Dad," I say, staring at the carpet.

"Then what's bothering you? Is someone teasing you at school?"

Everyone's teasing me at school, I think. *And it's only going to get worse when I turn up in these cheapo shoes.* But that's the least of my problems right now. I decide to give Dad one last chance to tell me the truth. This is it. If he lies to me about something this important, then I'm never trusting him ever again.

"That woman I saw you arguing with in the library," I begin slowly, glancing at Dad to see how he'll react. "She—"

"I told you, Norah," Dad says quickly, "she was just someone who wanted to use the computer at the same time as me."

"Right." I mutter. "So she didn't give you a business card with her phone number on it, then? The one that I found when I put your jeans in the washing machine?"

"Oh, that…" I can almost see the little wheels inside Dad's head working at double speed. "OK…"

Dad takes a deep breath and I lean forward eagerly. He's finally going to tell me the truth about my mother!

"I didn't want you to be upset if I told you who she really was," he says. "Sandra works for social services along with Linda and Kathy. She's the one who let them know we were staying with Ed and got us investigated. The day you saw us in the library, she was threatening to take you into care if I didn't get a job." He sees my eyes go wide, and he rushes on, "But that's not going to happen, ever! I won't let them take you away, and I've got everything sorted with Linda and Kathy, so you've got nothing to worry about, alright?"

I'm staring at him with my mouth open, but it's not for the reason he thinks. "And what about the Rainbow Children's Centre?" I ask. "The place she works at?"

"Oh, that? It's…um…it's a care home for children. But you won't ever be going there. Just forget all about her, Norah, it was a misunderstanding. But I've got it all sorted out now, and we'll be together forever, just you and me, OK?"

He gives me a hug, and I press my face into his jacket so he can't see the tears of disappointment forming in the corner of my eyes. I can't give up yet, though, or I'll never have the guts to bring it up again. "What about the photos?" I say it fast before I lose my nerve.

"The photos? What photos?" Dad's smile freezes, and now it looks like a grimace of pain.

"The photos in the box in your suitcase. I found them the other day when we were packing to go to the hostel. That woman Sandra's in them."

Dad gives a big fake laugh. "No, that's not her. It doesn't even look anything like her!"

"Who is she then?"

"Um…just someone I used to know."

"A girlfriend?"

"Sort of…yes." Dad's squirming uncomfortably in his chair and scratching the back of his neck. I'm not letting him off that easy.

"There was a picture of a baby too."

"Oh, yeah, she…er…she had a baby and I visited her in the hospital with some flowers. It was a long time ago. Before you were born. I haven't seen her in years."

Dad's lying to my face, and he isn't even blinking. There's no way I'm going to get the truth about the woman in the photo from him now. He's the one person in the world I thought I could trust, and finding out I can't feels worse than a hundred knives stabbing me in the heart all at once. Luckily the sales guy comes back with the shoes in my size and Dad goes to pay for them, so he can't see the tears in my eyes.

I want to go straight back home to take the photos out of the box again and show them to Dad so I can prove I know he's lying, but he stops at the supermarket first cos he wants to see if there are any bargains. I just can't face walking round with him and a basketful of out-of-date food with big yellow "reduced" stickers on them in case I see anyone from school, so I tell him I'll wait outside. Dad looks up at the sky with a frown. "It'll start raining any minute, pet. At least come and wait inside."

"It's fine. I'll come in if it rains."

Dad throws me a sad look as if he knows things are somehow broken between us and he doesn't know how to fix it, but he goes to find something cheap for our dinner anyway. At least the emergency loan means we won't have to go back to the foodbank. Dad was totally humiliated when he came to pick me up after that day in the park and he saw who Adam's mum was. She's one of our church busybodies who tuts and rolls her eyes if anyone walks into the service late and who tells the children off for eating too many biscuits at the coffee club. She helps out at the foodbank too—we've seen her there, but we've never spoken to her before. Now we'll never be able to go back to church without dying of embarrassment if we see her, and I won't be able to go to Sunday school and colour in pictures of my favourite Bible stories. Adam's mum has ruined everything.

I wander down the street a bit, swinging my shoe bag and staring in the shop windows. The shops get more expensive the closer I get to the park and the posh bit of town, and I'm just about to turn and head back to the supermarket when something in a perfume shop catches my eye. A shop assistant's talking to a man dressed in a fancy suit, but that's not what makes me stop and look. There's a girl in the shop the same age as me but taller, and she's hanging around the perfume testers, pretending to read the labels on the boxes. As soon as the shop assistant's back is turned, she suddenly swipes a bottle that's almost full, stuffing it into her bag along with its box. Then she walks straight out, her head down. She's so busy staring at the ground, she nearly runs straight into me.

"Norah! What are you…?" Chelsea Mackay stares at me with her mouth open, her cheeks going bright red. She knows I've seen her. She knows I've just figured out her big secret. "Look, it's not what you think!" she splutters, trying to hide her bag behind her back. "Please don't tell—"

"Norah, there you are!" Dad comes hurrying up. It's started to rain again, and the water's running down the street in rivers, soaking right through to our socks. "Let's get back before we drown."

I turn round to tell Chelsea Mackay she'd better give me my bike back or I'll tell everyone her secret, but she's already running across the road, meeting up with one of her foster brothers. It's my turn to stare at the ground and pull my hood up so he doesn't see me. I could tell Dad the truth about my bike and get him to sort it out with them, but I don't trust Dad to fix anything anymore. I'll sort it out myself with Chelsea when I see her in school. Dad's not the only one who's been lying to me. Chelsea won't be able to pretend anymore after what I just saw.

I splash through the puddles with Dad all the way back to the hostel, ignoring his attempts to get me to talk about school and about whether I want a cheese roll or a Pot Noodle for dinner tonight. I just want to go straight to that suitcase so I can pull out the photos and show Dad the writing on the back so he can't lie to my face anymore. But when we get to the hostel he makes me go straight into the bathroom to dry my hair and change my clothes cos he says he doesn't want me catching a cold. Huh, he sounds just like Adam's mum, only not nearly as posh.

When I come out wearing another pair of jeans and a dry jumper pulled over my T-shirt, Dad's on his phone, arguing with someone at the other end. My heart skips a beat, and for a second I think it's Sandra, the woman from the photo. But then I hear Ed's slimy voice and my heart sinks instead. I know what Dad's going to say even before he hangs up.

"I need to go out for a bit, pet. Ed needs a hand with something. Are you alright fixing yourself a Pot Noodle?"

"Yeah, I guess. But Dad—"

"See you later then—don't open the door to anyone while I'm gone, OK?"

Dad heads out before I can find the photos and call him out for lying. I pick my jacket up and hang it on the back of the door so it drips dry, and that's when I notice the suitcase in the corner is open. It's the suitcase that I found the photos in. I run over to check the box.

"No!"

They're gone. All of them. All that's left is Dad's newspaper clipping about his football matches. That why Dad made me go straight to the bathroom, so he could take them away. I should never have put the ones of mum back in there, I should've just hung onto them. Now all the evidence is gone, and Dad can lie to my face as much as he likes, cos there's no way of proving he isn't.

Not unless I just call her, I think.

No, I can't do that. What would I say?

Then why don't you go and see her? You know where she works.

Grimsby's across the river! I'd have to take the bus across the bridge, and I don't have the money.

Adam gave you money.

It might not be enough for the bus fare. And even if it was, the driver would never let me on the bus on my own. Anyway, that money was meant to buy food for Lady.

As soon as I remember the cat, I go running to the cupboard to fetch a bowl. Where I hid her was safe and dry, but she might have had her kittens already, and she'll be hungry. That's more important right now than my problems. I put my jacket back on and stuff the door keys in my backpack along with the bowl, hoping I can make it back before Dad does. I don't have an umbrella, but I trudge to the shop on the corner with my hood up, keeping my head down against the driving rain.

I buy a small carton of milk and a big packet of cooked ham, feeling a bit bad I'm paying full price for them. I didn't tell Dad about Adam's money. I was worried he'd take it straight to the betting shop, and tonight he's just proved me right. That'll be where he is right now, putting our emergency loan on the horses or in the fruit machine, and pretending Ed's the one with the gambling problem. I'm so angry at the thought of that I nearly trip over something that's sitting waiting for me on the pavement outside the shop.

When I look down, my heart nearly jumps out of my chest with joy. There's a small white dog twisting himself round my legs, whining and wagging his tail so hard his whole body's shaking. He's soaking wet and looks hungrier than ever, but Bingo's found me and I'm never going to leave him behind ever again.

"Good boy!" I pat him all over, then I give him half of the ham in the big packet. He gobbles it down like he hasn't eaten in forever, licking my fingers when he's done. I can't take him back to the hostel, but there is somewhere else I can bring him where it's safe and warm. Lady isn't going to like it, but she's just going to have to learn to share.

"Come on, Bingo. Come with me," I tell him. He runs after me like he'd follow me to the Moon. It's hard keeping out of the puddles as the gutters are overflowing with water and the pavements are like a mini river, but we manage to get to the old closed-down bingo hall without either of us drowning. I look around to make sure no one's watching, then I bend down and lift up the loose piece of wood over the bottom of the smashed glass door.

There's just enough room for me and Bingo to wriggle through.

It's dark inside, and I have to switch on the headlight—that's the only bit of my bike I have left. Dad and me used to go to the cinema when I was little and we had some money, and he used to say the posh name for a ticket hall is a "foyer". There's nothing posh about this foyer, though. The double doors to the big hall beyond are locked tight, the ticket desk is covered in cobwebs, and the posters round the walls advertising the prizes on offer are hanging in tatters. But it's dry and it's safe in here, and that's all that matters.

"Lady? Are you in here?" I call. My voice echoes round the empty room. A loud meow comes from under the ticket desk, and when I go to look I see Lady curled up there with a pile of fluff round her belly. Only it isn't fluff. It's five little kittens, all snuggled up and fast asleep.

Lady hisses when she sees Bingo, but before she can get her claws out, he starts licking her all over, his big rough tongue stroking all the fight out of her. She decides pretty quick that she likes that and he's not a threat, and she lets him curl up next to her and share the warmth. It's weird, I thought they'd fight for sure, especially now she's got kittens, but maybe she's just too hungry and weak. I pour milk into the bowl for her and she licks it up, being all dainty about it even though she must be really hungry. I guess everyone who comes from the posh houses round the park have nice manners, even the cats.

Lady does hiss at Bingo a bit when he tries to stick his tongue in her milk and eat the ham I give her, and that soon puts him in his place. He waits patiently till she's done, then I reward him with some milk and ham of his own. The little family looks so happy curled up there that I don't want to leave. But I don't have a choice.

I hurry away before Bingo can get up and follow me, squeezing out of the door again and pulling down the loose piece of wood so it looks like there's no way in. Then I pull my hood up against the lashing rain and splash away, back to the room that's not my own and the dad whose secrets have turned the two of us into strangers.

Chapter 18

ADAM

"Adam, can I come in?"

I sit up in bed, pretending to my father that I'm just sleepy from lying in too long, rather than wiping the tears from my eyes. I don't want to tell him about the nightmare I keep having of me drowning in the swimming pool while he just watches. I don't want to make him feel as terrible about it as I do. My father sits down next to me with the serious face he uses when he's talking to his clients over the computer.

"How are you feeling?" he asks.

I hesitate, not sure how to answer. I know he wants me to say I'm fine, so he can go back to work and ignore me again. But I don't want him to forget I exist, and I don't want him to keep arguing with my mother about whether I should go back to school or not. I just want things to be the way they used to be before I had cancer, and I have no idea what to say to make that happen.

"I'm tired," I mutter at last. That's true, at least. I haven't been out of my room in a week, not since my mother caught me and Norah in the treehouse and called the animal shelter. She wasn't happy when they turned up and found the cat gone, but I told her Lady ran out before I could stop her. I really hope Norah found somewhere safe for Lady to live, and I hope bringing a cat home didn't get her into trouble with her father. It sounds like she's got enough worries with all that crazy stuff about him pretending she doesn't have a mother.

Thinking about Norah and the fact I'll probably never get to see her again makes me so sad I have to give a big fake yawn and rub my eyes again like I'm sleepy, so my father won't see how upset I am.

My father sits on my bed, frowning at all the stuffed animals piled up there. He doesn't like them any more than I do. "Adam, it's not good for you spending so much time in bed," he says. He's being saying that a lot lately. But then he says something he's never said before. "I've been thinking—how would you like to get back to swimming? There are lessons at the local pool. I know your mother won't be keen on the idea, but I could take you on Saturdays, and I might be able to juggle my work schedule to get back early on Wednesdays too and take you to the five o' clock session. What do you think?"

I open my mouth to say, "I think that's amazing!" but then I remember how it felt to fall in the pond, and my dream of drowning and seeing my parents' terrified eyes as I slowly sank. Part of me is desperate to get back to the sport I loved, and part of me never wants to get back in the pool again. Part of me wants to take my father up on his offer, and part of me wants to keep my mother happy by staying sick at home so she doesn't get worried and argue with my father. I feel like I'm being torn in half, and whichever side I pick, I'm going to lose.

My father's sees the hesitation on my face, and he hands me some pages he's printed from the Internet. "I know you think being in hospital so long means you can't keep dreaming of the Olympics, but that's not true," he tells me. "Look, there have been other Olympic swimmers who've had leukaemia. There was Ikee Rikako, and the Dutch swimmer

Maarten van der Weijden—he won gold at the Beijing Olympics."

I look down at the news stories, my heart pounding with excitement. Maybe I can go back to swimming and get over my fear of the water. Maybe I can lose the weight I put on and get fit again. Maybe I don't have to give up on all my dreams after all! Maybe—

"Fraser!" My mother dumps a cup of hot chocolate and whipped cream down on my bedside table and snatches the printouts from my hands. "How many times are we going to go over this? Adam still has to take his maintenance chemo pills for another year and go for monthly check-ups. It's far too soon to be thinking about him going anywhere near a public swimming pool full of germs!"

"The doctors said swimming would be good for him!" My father stands up, his jaw clenching in anger.

"And I'm telling you it wouldn't!"

"Do you think you know better than the doctors?"

"Do you think the doctors are better at making decisions about my son's safety than I am?"

My father sees the scared look on my face as I sit there watching them yelling at each other, so he hustles my mother out, closing my bedroom door behind him. I can hear them standing out on the landing, their angry whispers carrying right through the door. The heavy knot of dread tightens in my stomach. My parents never argued before I got sick, or even when I was sick. They only started arguing when my cancer went into remission and I started asking to go back to my normal life. Maybe if I just pretend I'm happy not going to school and not going swimming then my father would accept that, and they would stop arguing. If they don't, they might end up getting divorced, and that would be all my fault.

I need to accept that I'm not going to get the things I want—the price I'd have to pay for them is too great. I need to do whatever it takes to stop my parents arguing, and that means doing whatever it is my mother wants. I unscrew the top of the bedpost and pull out the little piece of paper I've hidden there, tearing my list of all the things I want into such tiny pieces before I drop it into the bin that even if my mother finds it, she won't be able to read it.

There, it's gone. No more hopes. No more dreams. From now on, I'll just do whatever I'm told.

The front door slams, and I peer out the window to see my father's car pulling out of the driveway. Things with my mother must be bad if he's willing to go out in rain this heavy.

Before I can get out of bed and get dressed, my mother comes back in again and sits down next to me. Her makeup's smudged like she's been out in the rain, but I know it's because she's really upset and trying to put on a brave face. Now I have to be brave too, that way I'll never have to see the look of worry in her eyes I keep seeing in that awful dream.

"Adam, you know I only want what's best for you, don't you?" she says sadly.

"Of course I do, Mum."

"I'm not trying to stop you having a life. I just want to make sure you're fully recovered before we start thinking about things like school and swimming."

I nod, even though I know if my mother won't listen to my doctors, there's no proof in the world that will ever convince her that it's safe for me to live in the real world again.

"Once you're really better, I'll make sure you go to a good school, with friends you can trust— not like that girl Norah. She's a bad influence, Adam. Her father doesn't work, and I see them at the foodbank more than they're supposed to be. I heard a rumour that he's always at the betting shops and he has a gambling problem— you can see why I don't want you spending time with people like that, can't you?"

I shrug, hoping she'll take that as a nod as well. My mother's forcing me to agree with her that Norah's no good, even though she's wrong and she doesn't know anything about Norah. It's breaking my heart to be so disloyal.

You know the only way to fix your family is to do what she tells you, I remind myself before I say anything to defend Norah.

"And despite what your father says, I don't want to keep you locked up in here," she hurries on. "In fact, I phoned my sister last night. You remember your Aunt Alice, don't you? With the weather here being so bad, and you not being able to get fresh air out in the garden, I thought we'd drive up to stay with her for a few weeks. How does that sound?"

It sounds like the worst thing in the world. Aunt Alice lives in the middle of nowhere in the north of Scotland—her nearest neighbour is a half hour's drive away. My mother only wants to take me there as it'll be an even better prison than this house is. I don't say that, though. I know I should just agree to whatever she wants straight away, but I can't help looking for ways out of it first.

"But what about my medication and my hospital visits?" I try.

"Your next hospital check-up isn't for over three weeks, and we'll take your medication with us," she fires right back. I think she's already practised having this debate with my father. I try using him as an excuse next.

"Can Dad take a couple of weeks off work?" I ask. "I thought he'd already used up all of his holiday time?"

My mother hesitates, then smiles her too-bright smile that says she's not telling the whole truth. "Your father can't get the time off, so it'll just be you and me. But a bit of a change of scene will be nice, won't it? It'll be just like having an adventure."

My idea of adventure doesn't include staring out of Aunt Alice's cottage window at the grey skies and fields full of boring sheep for weeks on end, but I don't say that either. I'm all out of excuses, and if I want her to stop fighting with my father, I have to make it sound like I'm happy about everything she decides.

"It sounds great, Mum," I lie. "When do we leave?"

"We'll go on Friday," she smiles. It's a real smile of relief this time, and all the worry leaves her eyes, just like I hoped it would. "In the meantime…" she sets down a brightly coloured bag on my bed, and my heart sinks even further. I already know what's in it, and it's the last thing in the world that I want. "I know you were disappointed you couldn't keep that stray cat," she says, "but you know why you can't keep an animal full of germs, don't you?"

She keeps getting me to agree with her, and each time I nod, it's like I'm letting go of another piece of myself. Soon there won't be anything left of me to hold on to, and it'll be like my dream where eventually I can't fight the water anymore and I go sinking down to the bottom of the pool to drown. Maybe that wouldn't be so bad. Maybe at the bottom of the pool there's peace—no fighting, no worried eyes, just darkness and silence and all the guilt finally gone.

"Anyway, I thought you might like this." My mother pushes the bag towards me, and I open it with a heavy heart, pulling out the giant stuffed cat inside. It's ginger, just like Lady, and it would be perfect if I was three and a half instead of nearly twelve. "It's so lifelike, it's just like the real thing, isn't it?" my mother beams at me.

Just like the real thing. That's all my life is ever going to be—fake. Computers instead of friends, a tutor instead of schools, films and books instead of real experiences. It's time to finally just give up and accept it.

I sip the hot chocolate and whipped cream that's keeping me out of shape, hugging my mother's gift and smiling back just like she wants me to.

Chapter 19

NORAH

The pressure's been building up inside me all day, and one more little thing is going to make me explode. All of Dad's lies, the mystery of that woman Sandra who's probably my mum, the stress of not knowing what's going to happen at the end of next week when our stay at the hostel's finished—it's all swirling inside me like hot air in a balloon ready to pop.

I keep my head down in school, trying not to catch anyone's eye. I don't want the teachers asking me what's wrong, and I don't want any of the other kids thinking today's a good day to pick on me. I want to talk to Chelsea Mackay, to get her to give me my bike back now that I know her secret, but she's been avoiding me all day. She sticks to her best friends, Jenna and Yasmin, like glue, and there's no way for me to peel her off them so I can speak to her on her own about what I saw.

The art teacher makes me stay behind after the home-time bell to help clean out the paint trays, and by the time I get out to the playground, the parents have taken the younger kids home. Most of the kids from my year are still hanging out by the school gates, waiting for their turn at the ice-cream van that stops by at home time. Chelsea must've decided I'm too much of a coward to say anything about the other day, as she's got her new perfume bottle out, waving it around for all the girls to see and telling them how her mum sent it from New York.

When I walk past, she glares at me, daring me to open my mouth. I'm just about to tell her I want to talk to her on her own, when she smirks over at the boys on the other side of the road. Her foster brothers are waiting to pick her up from school. She thinks that threat's going to shut me up for good, and it nearly does, until I see they've also got their little foster sister with them. She's six years old, and she's sitting on a bike. A purple bike with silver stripes, stabilisers and a cargo box attached to the back.

That's when I can't hold it in anymore and the big angry balloon inside me finally bursts.

"You're a thief and a liar, Chelsea Mackay!" I yell at the top of my voice. "You stole my bike in the park, and you steal all your fancy perfume and expensive clothes from the posh shops in town!"

"Shut up, Norah-no-mates." Chelsea laughs nervously when all the other kids round the gates turn to stare. "You don't know what you're talking about."

"Yes, I do!" I shout back. I don't care who hears me now. "I saw you stealing that bottle of perfume from the shop. It's just a tester—it's not even new! I bet your mother doesn't send you anything, ever! She probably doesn't even live in New York or have a fancy job. She just moved somewhere far away so she doesn't have to see your ugly lying face ever again and that's why you're in foster care!"

It's the meanest thing I've ever said to anyone, and as soon as it's out of my mouth, I regret it. Chelsea's face goes chalk white and her mouth hangs open in shock like I've just hit her. Jenna and Yasmin exchange glances like they're not sure if they should try to stick up for her or not, but then one of the other girls reaches over and grabs the box Chelsea's got half hidden in her schoolbag.

"Hey!" the girl says, "Norah's right, this is just a tester—look at the label on the box!" She shows everyone before Chelsea can snatch it back, and all the kids in the mainstream class start laughing.

"Chelsea's a lying thief!"

"Hey Chelsea, I really want a pair of those new Nike trainers. Can you steal them for me next time you go 'shopping', or when your mother 'sends' you something from New York?"

"You're so lame, Chelsea. You're in foster care cos your mum doesn't want you."

"How come you two are hanging around with such a loser? Do you go shoplifting with her too?"

Jenna and Yasmin start backing away from Chelsea like they've just worked out she's caught the deadly disease of unpopularity, and they're scared she'll pass it on. The whole class is staring at her and laughing. Chelsea's bottom lip starts wobbling and a big fat tear runs down her cheek. Instead of making me feel good, it just makes me feel terrible.

Before I can say anything, Chelsea drops the perfume bottle. It smashes on the ground, and suddenly she's running so fast down the street her feet are just a blur in the giant puddles. She's gone before her foster brother can chase after her. I take off in the opposite direction before he works out her tears have got something to do with me.

I don't care about my bike right now. I don't care about anything except hiding away where no one can see me. I'm so ashamed of what I did to Chelsea I want to cry, but I'm angry too cos if Chelsea hadn't been so mean in the first place, then none of this would've happened. Then I'm mad at Dad, cos if he'd just had a job and a house like other dads, then we wouldn't have been scared of social services taking me away and I could've told him the truth about what happened in the park. Adam's mum was right— he shouldn't have left me there on my own. If he'd taken me to the park himself like other dads, instead of doing a rubbish zero-hours job that was pointless cos he just spent the money down at the betting shop with Ed, then I never would've lost my bike.

This isn't my fault, and it isn't Chelsea's fault either.

This is all Dad's fault.

By the time I make it to the bingo hall, I'm so out of breath I've got a stitch and my shoes and school trousers are soaking from running through giant puddles. The water from the overflowing gutter's swirling round the bottom step, and I'm glad the place has a fancy front entrance or the water would be getting in under the door by now. When I reach for the loose plank Bingo goes mad, scrabbling at the other side cos he can't get out to see me, and when I finally squeeze through the gap he jumps all over me and licks me like I'm a human trampoline made of ice cream.

"Calm down, you daft dog! Did you think I wasn't coming back?"

I don't like having to shut Bingo in here in the dark, but it's better than him being out in the pouring rain. I give him one of the sandwiches I kept from my school lunch, but I make sure Lady gets all the tuna from the other one even though he pinches the bread. I share the carton of school milk between them, then I sit back and watch the kittens that are fast asleep on Lady's belly. I don't try to touch them, and not just because Lady's got sharp claws. Bingo's got all protective of the kittens, and he doesn't like me getting too close to them either.

Once the milk's finished he curls up next to Lady again, taking turns to lick her ears and then lick my fingers. I wish I could stay there with them, but now that Dad doesn't have a job again, he's back to filling out job applications in the library. If I don't get there soon, he'll be suspicious about where I've been. He might think I've gone to see Adam, even though he's told me never to go to Adam's house again. He was so humiliated by Adam's mum telling him he wasn't looking after me right, he wouldn't forgive me if I went back there. He said Adam's mum's probably spread gossip about us round the church, so we haven't been back there either. Even though I miss the Sunday school and I miss the biscuits at the coffee club, I'm glad we don't go to church anymore, cos now Dad can't find out that Adam's mum caught me in his treehouse and sent me packing a second time.

I'm the one who can't forgive *him*, though.

If I had anywhere else to go, I'd run away right now and never come back, not even if Dad got a proper job and a nice house. Not after all the lies he's told me.

I put the plank back over the door and hurry down the street, wishing the stupid rain would stop. The heating in the hostel broke at the weekend, and I haven't had dry clothes to wear in days. Maybe I should use the rest of Adam's money to get myself a proper umbrella that doesn't blow inside out the second I put it up like the cheap ones from the pound shop.

There's a big golf umbrella in the window of the charity shop. I stop and pull what's left of Adam's money from my pocket, counting up the coins. It takes me ages as I'm rubbish at counting, but I've mostly got pound coins so I figure it out in the end. The golf umbrella's £4.50, and I've got £5.20, so that's enough. It's a lot of money to spend on one thing, especially as I'm supposed to be buying food for Lady and Bingo, but I'm sick of being wet all the time. I'll tell Dad my teacher lent it to me. He'll believe that.

I'm just about to go in and buy it, when I catch sight of the inflatable boat. It's still sitting in the corner of the window with its little price tag attached. My eyes light up, and I can't stop the mad idea that goes charging through my head. I'm too scared to call Sandra on the phone and ask her if she's my mum. Anyway, I'd have to use Dad's phone. He's never got any credit as he always wastes it calling the benefits line to sort out their mistakes, and he'd go nuts if he found out from the call log that I'd phoned Sandra.

But what if I went to see her?

Once I've bought some more food for Bingo and Lady, I don't know if I'll have enough money left for the bus over the Humber Bridge. But what if there was another way for me to cross the river? What if I had a boat and I could sail down the Humber to Grimsby to see the woman I think might just be my mother? What if that was the way I could finally find out the truth about why Dad's been lying to me all these years?

Before I can change my mind, I take a deep breath and open the shop door.

Chapter 20

ADAM

"Can't you come with us, Dad?" I asked for the hundredth time as my mother bundles me into the car.

"It's better if I don't," he says sadly as he lifts my suitcase into the boot. He doesn't say "I can't come as I'm working", or "I can't come as I don't have any holiday time left". That means he's not coming because he's fallen out with my mother. If I can't find a way to fix things, then they'll probably get divorced, and I can't stand the thought of that. But how am I supposed to put our family back together when I'll be stuck way up in the middle of nowhere with my mother and Aunt Alice, and my father's here at home all on his own?

"Are you sure you can't come after what we saw on the news last night?" I plead. "Now that the Humber's burst its banks and Hull's under so much water, it isn't safe to stay here anymore."

"The flooding won't affect this part of town, so don't worry about me, Adam. You just concentrate on getting yourself better so that when you come home you can get back to—"

"We need to go," my mother interrupts before my father can mention me going back to school or swimming again. "It's a long drive, and I want to drop off this food at the church first. Reverend Johnson says the hall's been turned into a temporary shelter for all the families whose houses have been flooded, so they need all the help they can get."

Our car's already stuffed full of food, blankets and packs of loo roll, and there's hardly any room for me in the back. It looks like we're taking our entire house on holiday with us, but it's mostly stuff to donate to the church. At least once we drop it off I might be able to breathe without my mother's giant pot of home-cooked chilli poking me in the ribs.

My father gives me a quick hug, and my mother drives off before I can tell him how much I'm going to miss him. I try to wave to him through the window, but the rain's falling so fast I can't see anything except a blur through the wash of water.

The roads are way busier than I thought they'd be considering how bad the weather is, but I guess everyone's trying to get out of the city to escape the floods. Apart from giant puddles, the streets aren't too bad on our part of town, but once we pass the shops my mother has to slow to a crawl, trying to keep the churning water from stalling our engine. The overflow's swirling under all the shop doors at the far end of the main street, and I can't even imagine how bad it must be for all the houses and shops that are way closer to the river than here.

Luckily my mother's church is up a hill, so the car park's dry and the road up north from here should be clear.

"You stay in the car and keep warm, Adam," my mother tells me, getting out and putting up her umbrella. "I'll get some of the church volunteers to come and pick up our donations."

She hurries over to the main entrance where I can just make out groups of people milling about inside the church foyer through the glass doors. I'm squirming around, hoping the volunteers won't take too long or I might just be squashed to death by my mother's cooking, when a taxi pulls up by the side of the church. A man and a small girl get out, pulling out suitcases and bags that look like they're already soaking wet. Just before they hurry to the small side door leading to the church hall, I recognise the girl's dark hair.

It's Norah!

Before I know what I'm doing, I've already jumped out of the car and run to the side entrance, calling her name. The rain's too heavy for her to hear me, and I have to go inside to find her. I stop just inside the doorway, amazed at what I see there. The hall's packed with people on chairs, mattresses and camp beds, and the place looks more like one of those refugee camps I've seen on the news than somewhere you'd go to Sunday school. I can't see my mother, which is good as it means she'll be busy ordering people about in the kitchen, but I do see Norah. She's sitting on one of the chairs, wrapped in a blanket clutching a cup of something hot, and her dad's on the other side of the hall talking to a group of parents.

I push my way past huddles of people, tripping over soggy belongings and squeezing my way through the crowd, until at last I'm sitting down next to Norah. I can't help giving her a hug. She looks like she needs it.

"Adam! What are you doing here? Your house isn't flooded too, is it?"

"No, my mother's taking me up to Scotland to stay with my aunt," I tell her, feeling terrible that I'm able to escape all of this while she's stuck here. "What happened to you?"

"The river burst its banks and our hostel flooded last night," Norah shudders. "You should've seen it—it was like one of those disaster movies. The water was running right down the hall and under the doors, and all of our stuff got soaked before we could carry it upstairs. We stayed in the second-floor corridor all night, and then we had to come here as there weren't any more rooms free."

"That sounds awful!" I feel even worse when I think about how I spent last night sound asleep in my nice warm bed and barely even heard the rain hammering against the window. OK, so I had the dream about drowning again and woke up in a cold sweat, but it sounds like the real-life nightmare Norah had to deal with was way worse. "What are you and your father going to do?"

Norah shrugs, looking small and helpless. I wish I could help. I wish there was some way to talk my mother into letting Norah and her dad stay at our house with my father till she has somewhere else to go, but even if my father agreed to that, my mother never would. Not after all the things she said about Norah's father being a gambler and them being a bad influence. All I can do is give her hand a squeeze.

"I'm sure you'll get a new room tonight," I try to reassure her. "One of the hotels will—"

"Ssh!" Norah says suddenly, squeezing my hand back so hard it hurts. She's staring at the big projector screen where someone's set up a computer so everyone can watch the news. Most of the people in the hall are too busy talking to pay any attention to it, and anyway they don't need the BBC to tell them that Hull's flooded, but Norah's staring at the local news report with wide eyes. I can just about make out the presenter's voice above the loud buzz of conversation around us.

"...although there have been no reports of casualties linked to last night's flooding, police are still looking for twelve-year-old Chelsea Mackay, who has been missing since yesterday afternoon. Last seen leaving school after three p.m., Chelsea didn't return home and hasn't made contact with her foster family. Police now fear after the devastating flood caused by the Humber bursting its banks, that—"

"Poor kid!" a woman says loudly behind us, drowning out the rest of the news story. "I always felt sorry for her."

"Did you know her, then?" An old man clutching a steaming mug of tea shuffles closer in his chair to hear her over the loud chatter.

"I knew her mother was no good. They used to live in the downstairs flat years ago when I was at Rathgate Close. Always had friends over at all times of the night, making her little girl play out in the hall so she wouldn't get in the way. She'd be at the bingo every night too—you know the one down by the Costrite supermarket? Couldn't bring her kid in, so she'd make her sit outside and wait for her till she was done. Never sober, but never seemed short of money either. Turns out she had a side business stealing from expensive shops and selling the goods on. Got five years for it, last I heard. No wonder her kid ended up in foster care."

Norah turns really pale, and I start rubbing her hand as I'm scared she's going to pass out. "What is it? Do you know what happened to that girl?"

Norah gulps hard and nods.

Chapter 21

NORAH

"Norah! Where are you going?"

Before Adam can stop me, I grab my backpack and race for the door. The guilt about telling everyone Chelsea was a fake and making her cry in front of half of our class has been eating me up, and now I'm feeling so sick about it I can barely breathe. Just before I make it out of the side door, Adam grabs my arm, pulling me back.

"What's going on? Isn't that the girl who took your bike?"

"Yeah, and it's my fault she ran away! I was mean to her in school, and—"

"*You* were mean to *her*? Norah, she bullied you and got her foster brothers to hurt you and push me in the pond. If you said something nasty, then she got what she deserves."

"You don't get it!" I snap, trying really hard not to cry. "What I did was way worse. I told everyone her big secret—that her mother wasn't really doing some fancy job in New York and sending her expensive gifts, and that Chelsea was just stealing stuff from shops and lying about it."

"Oh." Adam looks at me like he can guess where this is all heading.

"She was so ashamed she ran away, and that's my fault! I should've just kept my big mouth shut."

"She made you do it, so this is on her," Adam says, sticking up for me even though I don't deserve it. "But where are you going? Do you know where she is? If you do, we should tell the police and—"

"I've got no idea where she is!" I shake my head, wishing all the guilt and anger fizzing inside me would just go away. "I can't help her, but I can make up for what I've done by saving others who need me right now."

"Who?"

"Bingo and Lady. I hid them in the old bingo hall that woman was talking about, and that bit of town's flooded so badly the shops are all knee-deep in water. Lady's had her kittens, and if I don't go and save them they're going to drown!"

"Then we should tell some of the adults—your dad, or the church volunteers, or—"

"They won't help! They'll say it's too dangerous just for a dog and a few cats. You know what grown-ups are like, Adam, they never know what's really important."

He doesn't argue with that, but he's still not letting go of my hand. "What about the army?" he tries. "They rescue pets, I've seen it on the news. We could tell them and they could take one of their big boats over."

"I heard my Sunday school teacher say the army won't get here for another couple of hours cos they're busy dealing with even worse flooding up in Yorkshire. It has to be me, there's no one else who'll help Bingo and Lady. I've got a blow-up boat in my bag with my bicycle pump, and if you tell anyone and get them to stop me, I'll never forgive you, Adam, never!" I shake off his hand and go running out into the rain.

I get halfway down the hill, splashing through the puddles like my life depends on it, when I hear footsteps behind me.

"Norah, this is crazy! I can't let you do this!" Adam's running after me, his jacket and trousers already soaking.

"Go back to the church," I tell him without slowing down. "If your mother finds out you're outside, then she'll—"

"I'm so *sick* of my mother!"

Adam yells it so loud I nearly fall over in shock. That makes me stop. His face is bright red, and it's not just from running.

"All she ever does is make bad decisions and tell me it's for my own good. If she'd just let me keep Lady, then you wouldn't be out here right now putting yourself in danger trying to save her!"

I don't interrupt and tell him that, yeah, actually I would still have to save Bingo as I'm not allowed a pet either. Adam looks like he's about to burst with anger if he doesn't let it all out, and I know exactly how that feels.

"If she'd let me be friends with you, then you wouldn't have had to lie about your bike and you could've got it back! If we were friends, then she'd let you and your dad stay at our house so you didn't have to sleep in a crowded church hall that looks like something from a war film! This is all her fault!"

Huh. I thought this was all Dad's fault. Either way, grown-ups suck, and it's down to me and Adam to save our pets. "I have to get Bingo, Lady and the kittens, I just *have* to. Are you coming to help me, or are you going to Scotland with your mother?"

Adam closes his eyes like he's making the hardest choice of his whole life. When he opens them again, he doesn't look confused anymore, just determined. "I'll help you, Norah. Let's go."

We run down the hill together, splashing across roads like mini rivers till we get to the part of town where everything is so far underwater it looks like the shops are drowning. The bingo hall is at the far end of the street, but we can't get anywhere near it without wading up to our necks in ice-cold water. It's time to get my boat out and pray it doesn't have any holes in it, cos my puncture repair kit got left in my cargo box, and just like my bike, it's long gone.

Adam helps me unfold the plastic boat, and we take turns blowing it up with the pump. It's harder work than I thought it would be. By the time the sides start to thicken up, my arms feel like I've been carrying heavy bags from the foodbank the whole way across town.

"You think that's enough?" I ask Adam when he pulls the pump out and closes the valve.

"It'll have to be, I can't get any more air in." He looks round the street like he's hoping a grown-up will come along and ask us what we're doing so we don't have to go through with it, but it's completely deserted, and everyone's escaped to the drier bits of town. It's just me and Adam, and a plastic boat we don't even know will float.

"Ready?" I ask.

Adam nods, but when he holds on to the side of the boat so it won't get carried away while I clamber in, he looks a bit sick. The boat rocks from side to side when he gets in too, and the plastic bottom sags pretty deep into the water. I don't think this thing was meant for harder work than the inflatables session at the swimming pool, but it's too late to think about that now. The current catches us before we can change our minds, and we're swept away down the street.

"We have to stay close to the shops so we can catch hold of a door handle or a lamp post if we have to!" Adam yells, looking every bit as terrified as I feel. "We need to paddle!"

"How? We haven't got any oars!"

"Use your hands, like this!" Adam leans over the side and starts doing a sort of doggy paddle in the water. I try to copy him, but my balance isn't too good, and a couple of times he has to grab me to stop me from falling headfirst into the deep river. That scares me pretty badly—I can't swim, and after seeing Adam flailing about in the pond like a drowning duck, I'm not so sure he can either even though he says he was a champion swimmer once.

"Is this the place?" Adam says suddenly, grabbing onto a lamp post so we don't float right past it. I almost missed it—the front steps are completely underwater, and the river's so high it's lapping right up against the boarded-up entrance.

"Oh no!" I wail. "It's too late. The foyer's flooded!"

"Help me reach the door!" Adam paddles hard against the current, and I do my best to help, fighting against the swirling water that's trying to carry us away down the street. We manage to get hold of the planks across the glass entrance, but the loose plank at the bottom of the door is way down under the water. I can just about reach it if I lean right over the side of the boat, but there's no way I can swim inside.

"How are we going to get in?" I ask, hoping Adam knows what to do. But he just shakes his head, his eyes going really wide. "You said you were a champion swimmer! Can't you swim down and get through the gap?"

"That was before!" Adam thumps his fist against the planks in frustration when he can't get any of the other ones loose. "I can't do it now. I can't do anything anymore. I'm no use to anyone."

"But…" I trail off, feeling so helpless I want to scream. Maybe Bingo and Lady and her kittens are still alive in there, waiting just out of reach to be rescued. The water's still rising, and if we can't get to them now, they're going to drown for sure.

"Adam, can't you—"

"Ssh!" he suddenly snaps, leaning his head against the planks. At first I think he's mad at me, but then I realise he's listening to something from inside the foyer. "Do you hear that?"

"What is it?" I strain my ears, and a moment later I hear it too. It's faint and faraway, but it's very definitely the sound of someone calling for help.

"Someone's in there!" Adam gasps. "It's not just Bingo and the cats. Norah, we have to help them!" He's already kicking off his shoes and pulling off his jacket and heavy jumper.

"How?" I gasp. "If we can't swim down to the loose plank then—"

"I have to try. Give me your bike headlight, I'll need that to see when I get inside. Can you hold on to the door long enough to stop the boat floating away?"

I nod, feeling suddenly determined. If Adam can be brave, then so can I. I grab the other wooden boards across the door, wrapping my arms around them and holding on with all my might to keep the boat steady. Adam takes a deep breath, and before I can say anything else, he slips over the side of the boat and disappears.

"Wait!" I yell. I didn't even get a chance to wish him luck or tell him to be careful.

It's too late.

Adam's gone.

Chapter 22

ADAM

I'm halfway through the gap in the door when the fear hits me so hard, I nearly lose control of my breath and take a mouthful of water. All my bravery leaves me, and I'm no longer a champion swimmer who can power across a pool faster than a speedboat. Now I'm just an overweight boy who had leukaemia and can't even swim underwater for ten seconds without having a panic attack.

I try to reverse out of the hole in the door to get back up to the boat, but the gap's too narrow and the water's pressing down on the loose plank, pinning me in place. I'm trapped, I can't breathe, and I'm running out of air. My heart is pounding, my head spinning. It's dark under the water, but in my mind all I can see are the lights of the swimming pool above me and my parents' anxious eyes filled with tears as they stand there watching me drown.

This is it. My last moment on Earth. I'm never going to get the chance to go back to school, to make new friends who I can play football with, to be an Olympic champion or even just have a pet. I'm going to drown down in the dark, just like my nightmare told me I would.

No one can help me. Not my parents, my doctors—not even Norah. I'm all alone.

That's when I realise that if I want to live, if I want a chance at the life I always wanted, then I have to be the one to save myself.

I grab hold of the door frame, fighting against the weight of the plank and pulling myself through. My feet kick hard behind me, propelling me through the water and tearing the loose board right off. I'm finally free, no longer flailing helplessly but cutting through the water with determined strokes, just like I used to. I surface inside the foyer, taking great lungfuls of the dusty air and treading water till my heart stops pounding and my head clears.

I did it. I dug deep and found the part of me that cancer couldn't reach, the part I thought I'd lost forever. But leukaemia, the chemo drugs and even my parents being overprotective couldn't destroy my love of swimming. I'm a natural, and now that my gift's saved me, I'm going to use it to save others.

I pull Norah's headlight from my pocket, switching it on and shining it round the abandoned entrance room. The shouting starts again straight away.

"Over here!" a girl's voice calls. "Help! We're over here!"

Someone's sitting on the ticket desk. The water's so high it's swilling round the cabinets, and if the rain keeps pouring it won't be long till the whole foyer's flooded.

"Stay there. I'm coming to get you!"

I cross the distance in a few powerful strokes, all of my old confidence returning. When I pull myself up onto the ticket desk, I gasp in surprise. Chelsea's sitting there soaking wet with Bingo in her arms, and Lady and her kittens are huddled beside her in an old waste basket to keep them together.

"Chelsea! What are you doing here?"

"How d-do you k-know wh-who I am?" Chelsea's freezing, and she stutters with the cold. She doesn't recognise me in the flickering lamplight, and now's not the time to remind her what her foster brother did to me.

"I saw you on the news. Come on, I'll help you swim out."

"I'm not leaving them!" Chelsea clutches Bingo harder, wrapping her other arm around the basket full of cats.

"Don't worry about them, I'll come straight back for them. I need to get you out of here first."

"You promise?"

"I promise." I give Bingo a pat and tell him to stay. He stands at the edge of the desk whining as Chelsea and I slip back into the water, but I leave the headlight on the desk with him, and I think he understands. Even if he doesn't, he doesn't want to leave Lady and her kittens, so he just barks as he watches me and Chelsea swim away across the foyer, trying to remind me to come straight back.

"We need to go underwater to get through the hole in the door," I tell Chelsea. Even though it's dark, I can see her eyes going wide with fright. She's managed to swim this far on her own, but convincing her to hold her breath underwater is going to be trickier.

"You can do it!" I encourage. "It's not far— the boat's just on the other side of the door, and I'll be right behind you the whole way."

"I can't! What if I get stuck?" Chelsea splutters. She's already getting tired treading water, and her courage is running out.

"You won't. I'll help you through. You have to go *now*, Chelsea. The water's still rising and we won't be able to save the animals if you don't do this."

Chelsea looks like she's close to crying, but she does her best to be brave anyway, taking a deep breath at the same time as me and plunging under the water. This time I'm not scared—I have a job to do. Even though it's so dark, I manage to guide Chelsea to the gap in the door, pushing her through and making sure she keeps going and doesn't back out. It's easier now I've kicked away the loose plank, but it still takes so long I'm almost out of breath when it's my turn. I don't risk surfacing for another breath again in case Chelsea's in trouble on the other side. I just wriggle through the gap right behind her, hoping Norah's managed to keep the boat from being swept away.

She has. I surface at the same time as Chelsea, helping her swim to the side of the boat and climb in. Norah's eyes nearly pop out of her head when she sees who I've brought back with me.

"Chelsea! What were you doing in there? Are you OK?" She wraps her jacket round the shivering girl, and even though it's soaking wet too, at least the hood keeps the rain off her face. Chelsea's teeth are chattering too hard for her to reply, so Norah looks to me for an explanation instead.

"I need to go back for Bingo and the cats," I tell her. "Chelsea's kept them out of the water. Give me your backpack, it's the only way to get them out."

Norah doesn't look too sure, but she takes the bicycle pump out of the bag and hands it over anyway. "Be careful," she warns. I'm not sure whether she's more worried about me or the animals, but I nod and tell her I will. Before she can say anything else, I put the backpack on and plunge under the water again. This time I know what to expect, and getting through the door is just like the underwater exercises from my swimming club that I aced every time.

It's harder on the other side, though.

The bike headlight didn't like getting wet, and it's gone out. The only thing I have to guide me in the dark is Bingo's loud barking that gets even more frantic when he realises I've come back. When I eventually make it to the ticket desk, he jumps all over me in joy, and I feel bad for what I'm about to do to him and the cats.

"I'm sorry about this, boy," I tell him, stuffing him into the backpack before he can protest. Lady's even harder to coax into the bag, and she keeps trying to climb out until I quickly put the kittens in next to her so she can see they're not being left behind. It's a tight fit, but I zip the bag up before any of them can wriggle out.

Finding the door again is not too difficult, the hard bit's keeping the backpack out of the water until I swim over to it. I can't risk opening it up to check on the animals in case they fall out, so all I can do as I dive down is hope this crazy plan's going to work and we're all going to get out of this alive. I have a bit of a scare when the backpack catches on the door frame and I think we're all going to get stuck, but then I manage to pull it loose and carry it up to the surface with me. It's even heavier now that it's wet, and I have to struggle to lift it over the side of the boat. But it's like my fear is giving me strength now instead of taking it away, and I find an extra level of effort that I never knew I had.

"Are they OK?" I hold my breath while Norah opens the bag. She's swapped with Chelsea, and now the other's girls holding on tightly to the door planks to keep the boat steady, even though her fingers are trembling with cold. Norah pulls Lady out first, checking her over with anxious eyes. The cat's drenched and couching up water, but she's still with us. Before Norah can reach in for the kittens, Bingo comes scrambling out, shoving all of the kittens out with him. They go tumbling to the bottom of the boat, crying and climbing over each other to get back to their mother.

We did it. They're all safe. Norah and I exchange grins while she wraps them in my jumper to keep them together. Norah can't swim and I nearly chickened out, but despite our faults, we've just proved we're the best animal rescue team Hull has ever seen. Now I might finally be able to convince my parents to—

"I can't hold on anymore!" Chelsea cries, her cold fingers suddenly letting go of the door planks. I haven't had a chance to climb back in yet, and I just manage to grab the side of the boat as it's swept away down the street, hanging on with all my might. I could swim to safety on my own, but if I let go of the boat now, Norah, Chelsea and the animals might get carried all the way to the overflowing River Humber, and then maybe even out to sea.

"Adam, what do we do?" Norah yells, trying to keep Bingo from panicking and falling over the side. "We can't steer this thing!"

"See the wall over there? I'll try to push the boat over to it. Grab hold when we get there!" I shout above the rain.

Up ahead, there's a low wall on higher ground that's kept most of the water from the supermarket car park. It's our best shot of getting back to dry land. Even though my legs are aching and my lungs are burning with effort, I kick against the strong current, pushing the boat as hard as I can towards the wall. Norah tries to help by paddling, and even though she's mostly just splashing water in my face, her determination stops me from giving up. We finally make it to the wall, and Chelsea and Norah grab onto it with both hands.

"We did it!" Norah gasps, her arms shaking as she pulls herself out of the boat and over the wall. "We actually did it!"

Chelsea's too cold to say anything, but I know she'd be grinning too if her teeth weren't chattering so hard. She hands the animals to Norah, who makes sure they're on dry ground before she helps Chelsea clamber over the wall too. Out of the corner of my eye I can see a car stopping and a woman getting out and running across the car park towards us, but suddenly I find my grip on the wall loosening. The bricks where I'm holding on are crumbling, and for one horrible moment I think the current's going to snatch me away. I have no strength left to swim. If the flood gets me now, my nightmare will come true.

"Norah, help! I can't—"

Just before my head disappears under the water, a hand reaches out and grabs my arm, pulling me back up. The woman from the car's leaning over the wall, holding me under the arms and helping me to safety. I sit on the low wall for a long moment, coughing up water and looking at her in surprise. She looks a bit familiar, like someone I might've seen in a picture once, but it's Norah whose mouth's hanging open, staring at the woman in amazement.

"It's *you*!" she gasps. "You came to find me!"

"Norah, do you know this lady?" I ask.

"Yes." Norah takes a deep breath. "She's my mother."

Chapter 23

NORAH

Sandra's not my mother.

I know she isn't, cos the first thing she whispers to me when we're climbing into her car is, "I'm not your mother, pet. I'll tell you all about myself when I get you back to your father."

At least she didn't say that Dad isn't really my father, or that I was stolen from the hospital at birth. That's something, I guess, but it doesn't make the crushing blow of disappointment hurt any less.

When we get to the church there's a police car parked outside the hall, and I'm scared that we're going to be in big trouble till I see the look on Dad's face when he scoops me into his arms and hugs me tighter than he's ever held me in his whole life. Adam's mum and dad are both there too, and they look like they've been out of their minds with worry.

Everything goes a bit crazy after that, like someone's pressed fast forward on a film and it's hard to work out what's happening. The church hall has a little shower room in the back cos it sometimes puts up homeless people in winter. All three of us have to take a turn at scalding our skin off in there and then being wrapped in blankets while folk fuss about us, blow drying our hair and force feeding us way too many cups of hot tea.

Chelsea's foster family turns up while we're answering the police officers' questions about what we were doing. They look so happy to see her safe, it makes me think that maybe her foster brothers aren't such terrible people after all. The one who took my bike starts crying when he hugs Chelsea, even though he's about fourteen, and I almost forgive him for stealing my bike when I see that. They both look awkward when they realise it's me and Adam who rescued her, but I'm too busy making sure Bingo and the cats are OK to talk to them.

Some of the church volunteers have dried them all off, fed them and put them in a big cardboard box so they can't run away. Bingo looks like he's loving the attention, but Lady's hissing at anyone who gets too near her kittens, so I think I should probably leave them be for a bit. Now that I know they're safe, I have something even more important to worry about. Dad's standing in the corner having a big talk with Sandra. They're not arguing this time, but Dad's not looking happy. Finally they both seem to agree on something, and they come to sit next to me. They exchange glances like they're not sure who should do the talking, but I don't care as long as it's the truth.

"What's going on, Dad?" I ask. "Sandra says she's not my mum, but those photos said she was. You said I was a test-tube baby and I came out of a lab. You said I didn't have a mum!"

"You told her that?" Sandra frowns at Dad like he's told me he found me growing in a cabbage patch when I was a baby, and that doesn't make me feel any better about believing him for all these years.

"You know why I didn't want to tell her the truth, Sandra. This hasn't been easy on me, especially after everything you and your parents said during the lawsuit."

"We just wanted what was best for Norah." Sandra's frown's getting deeper, and I'm worried they're going to fall out again before I can get to the bottom of this.

"You never thought I was good enough for Stacey! And now you don't think I'm a good enough father, and—"

"STOP IGNORING ME!" I yell, shutting them both up. "Tell me the truth! Who's Stacey?"

Sandra takes a deep breath. "Stacey was your mother, pet," she says before Dad can stop her. "She was my twin sister. She died six months after you were born, and your dad and my family argued about who should bring you up. We ended up going to court about it."

"Oh." It's my turn to look stunned. "Why didn't you just tell me, Dad? Why didn't you tell me I had a real mother instead of making something stupid up?"

Dad stares at the ground, fiddling with his coffee cup like he's really embarrassed. "Because there were a lot of harsh words said on both sides while the court case dragged on, and when I got custody, I didn't want Stacey's family trying to take you away from me again."

"That's not what we wanted!" Sandra snaps. "We just wanted to spend time with Norah. You wouldn't even let us have that!"

"You always said I didn't look after Stacey properly!" Dad looks her in the eye now, his face going red. "But who was it who took care of her when she drank too much, hmm? That was me. I didn't see your family rushing to take her to hospital all those times she passed out or hurt herself falling down. You blamed *me* for her problems! You said if I was a better husband she wouldn't drink so much, and Norah wouldn't have been born with—"

Dad bites his tongue before he can say anything else. "Born with what?" I frown.

"Nothing, pet, it's just that it's not very good for a baby when its mother drinks a lot when she's pregnant. You were sick as a baby, and that's why you struggle with things like counting and reading now. But it doesn't mean there's anything wrong with you, don't ever think that! I mean, I'm not any good at reading either, am I? We're two peas in a pod, you and me, aren't we?"

Dad's desperate to make me smile at him like I used to and tell him nothing's ever going to come between us. But it feels like there's still an invisible wall separating us, and that's not going to come down till I understand everything there is to know about the past.

Sandra's the one who breaks the silence. "I didn't mean to blame you for Stacey's drinking," she sighs. "I know that wasn't your fault, I was just angry that I was her twin and I couldn't help her. Then when her post-natal depression got so bad that she drank herself to death, I felt so guilty at not being there for her, I blamed you for that too."

"She did WHAT?" I gape at them, my mouth flapping up and down. "You mean Mum was so sad after I was born, she didn't want to live anymore?"

Dad puts his arms round me before I can start crying. "It had nothing to do with you, Norah," he soothes. "She loved you more than anything, but she was very sick and she wouldn't let any of us help her. I tried, Sandra, believe me, I tried."

"I know you did, Ronnie. I'm sorry I blamed you all these years." Sandra reaches out and gives Dad's hand a squeeze. They both have tears in their eyes, and that makes me want to cry even harder.

"But why did you fight over me?" I ask. "Why couldn't I have lived with you both?"

"Sandra and your grandparents wanted sole custody of you. That meant I wouldn't have got to see you much, so I fought to make sure I was the one who brought you up," Dad says. "But I wasn't earning much, and then when I lost my job and we ended up homeless, I was worried they'd use that as an excuse to take you away from me."

"That's not what we wanted." Sandra shakes her head. "My parents and I just wanted to help out, and to see Norah. That's all."

"Wait, I have *grandparents*?" I stare at Dad and Sandra in amazement.

"You do, pet," Sandra smiles sadly. "And they're dying to meet you. What do you say, Ronnie? They've got space in the B&B they run in Keelby—it's not too far from Grimsby. Why don't you and Norah come and stay for a bit, just till you're back on your feet after the flooding. It would give Norah a chance to meet them, and they'd love to see her."

"I don't know," Dad frowns. "After the lawsuit and the way they tried to make me look like I was a bad father, and—"

"That's all in the past now. We know you've done your best for Norah. They just want to see their granddaughter, and I just want to see my niece and spoil her a bit like an aunt should."

"But—"

"Don't I get a say in this?" I say, thumping my tea mug on the table so they know I mean business. In the last couple of minutes my whole world's been turned upside down, and my head's still spinning. I'm still mad at Dad for lying to me, but I'm starting to understand why he did it. After all, I haven't exactly told him the truth about everything, have I? I lied about seeing Adam, cos I didn't want to lose his friendship, and I lied about what happened in the park, cos I didn't want Chelsea bullying me even worse in school. I even lied about keeping Bingo and Lady in case Dad called the animal shelter like Adam's mum, and because of that I nearly lost them in the flood. Maybe Dad's right—we're two peas in a pod, and we've been making exactly the same mistake by not trusting each other with our secrets.

"So, what do you want to do, Norah?" Dad says. "Do you want us to go and stay with your grandparents for a few days, or would you rather we left it till things are more settled here?"

"That depends," I say.

"On what?" Sandra asks.

"On whether they like animals or not." I glance over at the box where Bingo's whining. He's trying to scramble out to get to me, but the sides of the box are too high.

Sandra laughs. "You're just like your mother. She loved animals at your age too."

"Did she?" That makes me feel all warm and fuzzy inside. I'm not just like my dad—I had a real mum and I'm like her too even though I never got a chance to meet her.

"Don't worry—my parents live on a farm, and there's always plenty of animals to look after. A few more wouldn't make much difference."

"Really?" It's like Santa has come even though it's May, and instead of bringing me another bike, he's brought me an entire family complete with all the pets I could ever want.

Before I can burst with excitement Sandra says, "We'd better get going. It's still raining, and I don't want to be driving in it when it gets dark."

Dad nods and goes to get our suitcases that are stored in a big jumble of people's belongings by the far wall. I run after him when I realise there's still something I need to ask him. It's a hard question, but it's been eating me up inside for ages, and if we're going to have a fresh start, then I need it answered.

"Dad?" I grab his hand so I can look straight in his eyes and see if he's telling me the truth or not. "Will you promise me one thing?"

"What's that, pet?"

I take a deep breath. "Do you promise you won't gamble anymore? You won't go to any more betting shops and waste our money on the horses or the fruit machines?"

Dad looks like I've just grown two heads and told him I'm a mutant zombie. He blinks at me with his mouth open for a second, then he gasps, "Norah! Is *that* really what you think I've been doing with our benefits money?" He looks so disappointed that I start to feel terrible for even thinking it.

"But we never have any money!" I say, "And—"

"You know that's because the people in charge of handling our benefits claims keep getting things wrong. Linda and Kathy at social services are helping me to sort that out, so once our B&B bill's been paid, we won't be in debt anymore."

"But you're *always* at the betting shop!" I protest. "You spend more time there than you do at the job centre or the library, and you always come back looking so sad! So I thought…" I trail off, realising I've got yet another thing wrong, but this time it's cos I never bothered to ask what the real story was.

Dad crouches down so we're face-to-face and I can see the truth in his eyes. "Norah," he says seriously, "I haven't been gambling at all. I promise you I'd never waste a single penny when you've had to do without so much."

"Then how come you were always down at the betting shop?" I frown.

"Because I've been trying to keep Ed from gambling away all his money. He's got a wife and five kids to feed, and if I'm not there, he makes stupid bets and then his family don't get to eat. He doesn't always listen to me, but I thought maybe if I could help him with his addiction it would make up for not being able to help your mother with hers."

"What happened to her wasn't your fault, Dad. Aunt Sandra said so."

"I know, pet. But that doesn't mean I don't blame myself sometimes."

I give Dad a hug. He's been dealing with so much, and instead of helping him and believing in him, I've just been making things worse. "Can we promise not to keep secrets anymore?" I whisper in his ear.

"I promise, Sunny," Dad whispers back. "Now go and get that zoo of yours and we'll take it over to your grandparents' house before Sandra changes her mind."

It suddenly hits me that even though I can take Bingo and the cats, there's other people I'll have to leave behind. I go running across the hall, looking for Adam. He's finished talking to the police, and now his parents are about to take him home. I feel a bit shy talking to him in front of them, especially as his mum probably thinks I nearly got him drowned cos I'm such a bad influence, but she looks too relieved that he's safe to be angry.

"Adam! I have to go. My Aunt Sandra's taking me and Dad to stay with my grandparents for a few days on their farm in Keelby, and I can bring Bingo and the cats with me. They've told me everything about my mum! Well, not everything, but it's a start."

I beam at him and he grins back, but his smile's a bit sad. At first I think it's cos I'm taking the animals, but then I realise it's cos I might not see him ever again.

"Maybe you can maybe come and visit?" I say quickly. "Aunt Sandra says there's loads of room at their B&B."

"I don't think that's a good idea," Adam's mum says. "Adam needs to—"

"It's a great idea," Adam's dad interrupts, pulling out a piece of paper and writing down a phone number. "Call any time you like, Norah. It's about time Adam spent more time with people his own age."

"Thanks, Dad." This time Adam's smile's real, and he gives me a hug before his parents take him home. I wave through the glass doors till his car drives off, and then I'm just turning away to go back to the main hall when Chelsea's foster family come out. Chelsea looks really embarrassed, but her foster brothers come straight up to me while her foster parents finish talking to the police.

"We know what you did," one of them says. At first I'm not sure if it's some kind of threat, but then the other one says, "Yeah, thanks, Norah. You're alright."

They're staring at the ground and shuffling their feet, too embarrassed to look me in the eye. That's probably the best I'll get out of them. As apologies go, it's pretty rubbish, but then Chelsea finds the courage to come over too.

"Thanks for saving me, Norah," she says. She must really be related to her foster brothers, cos she's staring at her feet too, exactly like them.

"It was mostly Adam," I shrug, feeling secretly pleased. "He did all the swimming."

"Yeah, but he wouldn't have come looking for me if it wasn't for you. How did you know I was in the bingo hall?"

I should probably tell the truth about really just looking for Bingo and the cats, but now that me and Dad and Sandra have told so much truth already, one little white lie won't hurt, will it? Not if it makes Chelsea feel special.

"I heard someone say your mum used to bring you there when you were little, so I thought I'd take a look."

"That was smart. It's got happy memories of her, that old place. She always loved her bingo nights, and she was always in a good mood when she came out."

I don't know what to say to that. Chelsea's never said anything to me before that wasn't mean, and her being nice is going to take a bit of getting used to. Her cheeks are red with embarrassment, but she forces herself to look me in the eye. "I'm really sorry about your bike. And now I know it was Adam these two idiots shoved in the pond, I feel even worse." She thumps her foster brothers on the arm. "I'll give your bike back, I promise."

Chelsea's trying really hard to make up for what she did, and now it's my turn to make up for humiliating her in front of our class and making her run away. It isn't easy, but then real apologies never are. "Does your little sister like the bike?" I ask before I can talk myself out of it. I don't say "foster sister". I get now that she's Chelsea's family whether they're related or not.

"Yeah, it's a great bike, she plays on it all the time. But it's yours, so—"

"She can keep it," I tell her, squeezing my hands into fists so I don't start crying. I've just been given the gift of grandparents and an aunt and pets and a new place to stay. I don't need to be greedy. Chelsea's foster family don't have much money—if they had, Chelsea wouldn't have been trying to impress everyone with stolen stuff in the first place.

"Are you sure?" Chelsea looks at me doubtfully.

"Yeah. And I'm sorry about what I said in school."

Chelsea gulps hard and nods. "I guess we're even, then?"

"Yeah, I guess we are," I grin.

Chapter 24

ADAM

"What is it you really want, Adam?"

My mother and father sit opposite me on the sofa, and I fidget in my chair, feeling like I'm defending myself in a courtroom from one of those crime dramas. I'm not sure what to say. I don't want my parents to start arguing again, but I don't want life to go back to the way it was before me and Norah went on our rescue mission today either.

"Adam?" my mother asks again.

I take a deep breath and decide to do the one thing I should've done a long time ago. I tell the truth.

"When I was in hospital, the doctors said I should write a list of the things I wanted when I was well again," I begin, hoping I'm not going to make everything worse by being honest.

"Do you still have it?" my father asks.

"No, I threw it away weeks ago. I didn't think I'd ever be able to get what I wanted."

"But why not?" My mother looks upset. "You know we just want the best for you, and if there's anything you'd like you just have to ask."

"But that's just it, Mum!" I sigh. "What you want for me and what *I* want aren't the same thing! I tried doing the things I wanted, and it just made you and dad argue all the time."

Before my mother can protest my father says quickly, "What was on your list, Adam?"

"The first thing on my list was to go back to school. If I don't finish the term at a local school, then I won't have a chance to make any friends before secondary school and it'll be even harder if they all know each other."

My mother frowns and clutches her coffee mug so tight I'm worried it's going to shatter. My father tries really hard not to give her the "I told you so" look I know he's dying to give her, and says instead, "So how about it, Helen? We both know it's best for Adam in the long run."

My mother stares into her coffee, then gives a tight little nod. It's not much, but its meaning is so huge I have to fight the urge to run over and hug her. Not yet. There are still a few things on my list I need to negotiate first.

"The next thing on my list wasn't just for me," I say slowly, hoping my mother's not going to take this the wrong way. "But I thought if I go back to school, you could go back to work, Mum."

She looks up quickly, and I'm not sure if she's angry or not as her expression is hard to read. "I couldn't do that, Adam. You need me here. What if something happened at school? And who would pick you up after school? I should just stay at home."

I'd usually just let it go, but my mother's not sounding as decisive as she usually does when she tells me the way things are going to be. In fact, she's sounding half hopeful, almost like she wants me to change her mind. Her eyes have lit up, just like I know mine did when my father started talking about school and swimming lessons. Maybe I've had it all wrong until now. Maybe I haven't been the only prisoner in this house, and maybe my mother's felt every bit as trapped as I have. All that cleaning and cooking and endless busyness was just her way of crying for help, and I was too focussed on my own misery to see it. It's time we rescued each other and found a way out of this together.

"You could go back to work part time to begin with," I suggest, "just till I'm settled in school. If you find a job you like, maybe you could go full time once I'm in secondary school. There'll be loads of clubs and things I can do after school, so you wouldn't need to worry about getting home early every day."

"I'll have a think about it," my mother says, but this time she's smiling, and I know what she really means is, "Yes, that's a great idea!"

My father's grinning now too. I think he can probably guess what's next on my list.

"I know you weren't keen on me looking after the neighbour's cat," I keep going before I lose my nerve, "but I miss Benjy almost as much as I miss having friends. If I had a pet, I wouldn't be so lonely."

My mother's face falls as soon as I say that. "Oh, Adam, how can you say you're lonely? I've been here the whole time, and you've had your tutor almost every day, and—"

"But it's not the same!" I protest. "Meeting Norah was the best thing that's happened to me since I got ill, and now I might not ever see her again."

"Yes, you will," my father says. "We'll make sure of it, won't we, Helen?"

My mother bites her lip. "I suppose she is brave, after what she did for that runaway girl and those animals, though I do wish she hadn't dragged you into it, Adam."

"She didn't drag me into it, I volunteered. If I hadn't met her, I might have given up all my dreams completely and just believed I was sick for the rest of my life. If she calls, can I see her again, Mum, please?"

My mother nods, but she's crying now, and has to go and get a box of tissues. I feel bad that she's upset, but the weird thing is, I don't feel scared about her being anxious anymore and I don't feel guilty. It's like I've been underwater ever since I left the hospital, and I can breathe properly for the first time in ages.

"So, what kind of pet were you thinking of Adam?" my father asks, trying to distract us both from the sound of my mother blowing her nose noisily in the kitchen. "Another dog might be a bit of a handful if you're going back to school and your mother goes back to work."

"I was thinking of a cat," I say. "I wanted Lady—that's what I called the neighbour's cat—but I think she'll probably be staying with

Norah now. But she has kittens, and maybe if I took a few of them, then—"

"A few?" Dad's eyebrows nearly go flying up off his head.

"Well, maybe two…" I grin at him. I'm starting to get the hang of this negotiating for what I want.

"Was there anything else on that list of yours? A private jet? A pet elephant? Your own spaceship?" Dad's shaking his head, but he's laughing too. For the first time since I got out of hospital he's treating me like he used to—like I'm his best friend instead of a total stranger made of fragile glass who'll break if he even speaks to me—and that makes me feel like a million pounds.

"No, just the kittens," I grin back. "But now that you mention it, a spaceship would be pretty cool, especially if it had its own swimming pool."

"Then you do want to go swimming again?" Dad's smile turns serious.

"Do you think Mum would let me?"

"Let you do what?" My mother comes back in with the box of tissues. Her eyes are a bit red, but the worry lines that've been cutting deep into her forehead for ages look a lot more relaxed.

Dad looks at me, and I can tell he wants me to say it. He doesn't want it to look like he's pushing me into anything. I need to be brave one last time.

"I didn't write the thing I wanted most on my list, as I didn't think I'd ever get it."

Mum looks a bit worried, but she doesn't ask what it is. She already knows.

"I know you think swimming pools are full of germs, Mum, but I love swimming more than anything! The doctors say it's safe, and it'll be a really healthy way for me to lose weight. I'm sick of being unfit and just dreaming about the time I used to be good at something."

"But you're good at lots of things, Adam," my mother protests before I can get another word in. "You're good at writing and schoolwork, and you've read so many books that—"

"But swimming's my passion!" It's my turn to interrupt her. I'm not letting her talk over me and steamroller me into doing what she wants anymore. "You used to love watching me swim. You said it made you really proud."

"Oh, Adam!" Just as well that my mother's brought the tissues, as she looks like she might start crying again. "I didn't want you to think that swimming was the only thing that made me proud and that if you stopped doing it, I wouldn't love you as much anymore. I thought if you went back and struggled because the hospital treatment made you so out of shape, you'd start thinking you were a failure, and I couldn't bear the thought of that."

"So it wasn't just about the germs?" All this time my mother's been trying to protect me from the wrong thing. If we'd all just told the truth, we could've sorted this mess out months ago. It's like we've been floating around in a lifeboat on a stormy sea, and we've only just figured out we've all been rowing in different directions. Now we're all going the same way, and we might just be able to find the happy home we've been searching for after all.

"I know it'll be hard, and I might not be able to compete like I used to," I tell her, "but I want to try. Maybe I'll never be an Olympic athlete, but after helping Chelsea today, I've been thinking that I could be a lifeguard, or one of those lifeboat crew who save people in stormy seas, or..." I run out of breath, but with excitement this time. There are so many things I could do despite my cancer that I'm almost dizzy at the possibilities for my future.

"You can do anything you put your mind to, Champ," my father says softly. "We both believe in you."

Champ. My father hasn't forgotten after all. Maybe he was just afraid to say it in case it made me sad I wasn't swimming anymore. Hearing him call me that name makes me feel happier than all the trophies and medals I've ever won, as now I know no matter what happens, my father will always be proud of me.

He stands up and grabs the coffee cups to hide the fact that he's got tears in his eyes. "I'll just rinse these out. Anyone else starving? I can do us a quick stir-fry for dinner."

My mother blows her nose one last time and grabs the cups off him. She might be ready to go back to work, but she isn't ready to give up the kitchen just yet.

"I'll make roast beef and honey-glazed vegetables, and we can have sticky toffee pudding with whipped cream and—"

"*Mum!*" I groan. "I'm never going to lose weight if you keep cooking me giant meals. Can't we just have something simple?"

My mother looks disappointed for a minute, then I say something that makes her eyes light up.

"Please, Mum? I really need your help with this."

It's like I've found the magic words to turn her from the prison guard who's been making my life a misery into my own personal trainer.

"Of course!" she beams. "I can do roast vegetables instead, and you can have some fruit for dessert. Maybe after dinner we can all go for a walk together in the park."

"But it's still raining!" I look out of the window at the grey storm clouds, then back at her in amazement.

"We can bring our umbrellas. It's just a bit of water, Adam. It won't do you any harm."

She goes back into the kitchen to make dinner, and my father and I exchange secret grins.

Chapter 25

NORAH

Global warming's made the weather completely crazy. After the flooding, the weather got so hot they had hosepipe bans down in London, and even up here in Keelby, folk were talking about what a dry summer it was going to be. It rained a bit last week, though, so even though it's a really warm July day, the fields round my grandparents' farm are still green.

My grandparents. I still can't get used to saying that. Even though we've been here for two months, it still sometimes feels like I'm living in a fantasy where I've won the lottery. I don't mean that life's perfect or anything. They're not rich and they have to work really hard to keep the farm going, and Dad sometimes argues with them when he thinks I can't hear them. But Dad likes the work he does around the farm, and I like being around all the animals, and I like it when Aunt Sandra drives over from Grimsby for dinner. Most of all, I like being part of a family and hearing stories about the mother I never knew I had.

"Ugh, Norah, that's gross!" Adam says suddenly, interrupting my daydream.

I look down and see I've been letting Bingo lick the last of my ice lolly.

"He's just thirsty. And anyway, I let him try yours before I gave it to you."

Adam's eyes go bug-wide before he realises I'm just joking. He gives me a playful shove, and I nearly go tumbling off the little wall we're sitting on in the farmyard.

"Careful! If you break my neck, I won't ever ask you back."

Adam just shakes his head. He knows how desperate I've been for him to come and visit. We've been talking on the phone nearly every day since I moved here, but it's not the same as seeing him. He said that now school's finished for summer and his parents have taken a week off work they've got time to drive him over, but I think it's taken this long for his mother to realise that we're best friends and keeping us in different towns isn't going to change that. I think his parents were a bit surprised when they arrived at the farm this morning. I don't think they were expecting to see how big the house was, or the nice B&B attached to it. It annoyed me a bit at first that they're still judging me and Dad on where we live and how much money they think my family has, but at least they'd already decided to let Adam and me be friends before they drove down here.

"So, have you decided yet?" I ask, giving up and letting Bingo run off with my ice lolly.

Adam frowns. It's a hard decision, and it's not one I can help him make as I think every choice is perfect. "I was thinking the ginger one with the white paw, and the white one with markings on her face. They get on the best."

I nod. "The two girls—yeah, that's probably best." I don't think Adam's parents would be happy if he filled the house with more kittens a year from now.

"You don't think Lady will mind?" he asks.

"Are you kidding? As soon as they were old enough to do stuff on their own she started treating them like the kids at school used to treat me."

"But you said the other kids have been a lot better since the flooding."

"Yeah, sort of."

"Sort of?"

I pull up a long stalk of grass and chew on it, the way Grandpa Gibson does when he's working out in the fields. It tastes pretty yukky, but it makes me look like I'm thinking really hard.

"The other kids have just been ignoring me, which is good. It was mostly Chelsea who got them to pick on me, but now that she's been kicked out of the popular group and hangs around with me, that doesn't happen anymore."

"Are you two still getting on OK?" Adam asks.

I shrug. "I guess so. I thought she was just being my friend cos Jenna and Yasmine don't speak to her anymore, but she's actually nicer than I thought she was. I think she's happier now that she's not pretending to be someone she's not, and she's told me all about her mum and her foster family."

"So you're friends?"

I chew my grass harder and think about that for a bit, then I nod. "Yeah," I say at last. "We're friends." It's taken me a long time to forgive Chelsea for all the mean things she's said, and even longer to try to forget them, but she's been trying so hard I guess it's only fair that I make an effort too. Besides, I haven't decided which secondary school I'm going to yet, and if it's the one Chelsea's going to, it'll be nice to have a friend there.

I stretch out on the wall and stare up at the sky. It's so blue it looks like a swimming pool full of inflatable little clouds. That reminds me to ask about Adam's favourite hobby. "How's the swimming going? Are you still going to compete in that competition next month?"

It's Adam's turn to think for a bit before he replies. He lies back too, letting Bingo lick the ice lolly juice off his fingers even though he pretends it's gross.

"My mother's not keen on me competing as she knows I'll lose, and she thinks that'll put me off," he says at last.

"Will it?"

"Nope. I know how much training I still have to do to get fit, and how far behind the other kids I am. I think my father gets why I want to enter the competition, though."

I don't get why he wants to enter, but I don't want him to think I'm an idiot who can't work out what's going on his head either, so I just stay quiet till he says, "My father knows it's not about winning. It's about me beating myself."

"Beating yourself up?" I have no idea what he's on about.

Adam laughs. "No, I mean challenging myself to do better than I could do last month, or even last week. That's what swimming's about. Even just taking part in a competition is a big step forward from where I was six months ago."

"It's a big step up from where you were *four* months ago," I say without thinking. "You couldn't even get out of a duck pond back then without splashing about so much you drowned half the ducks."

At first I think Adam might not like being reminded of that, but then he laughs so hard he rolls off the side of the wall. "You've got the weirdest sense of humour of anyone I've ever met, Norah."

"Seeing as you've been stuck in your room half your life and you've only ever met about three people, that's not much of an insult," I throw right back, helping him brush the newly mown grass off his expensive jeans before his mother has a fit.

"Norah, Adam!" Grandma Gibson is standing at the back door calling for us. "I've made us all an early dinner!"

"Coming, Grandma!" I call back. *Grandma.* Wow. I'm never going to get bored of saying that. I never knew a single word could make me feel so warm and fuzzy inside.

We head back across the yard, stopping to pat Lady when she comes running up to us. I try not to notice that she's been hunting mice in the barn again. I've already rescued five in the big cage that Grandpa Gibson bought me, and I don't think I'll be allowed to keep any more. Luckily Lady isn't interested in insects, so she hasn't tried to eat the three big spiders that have woven giant webs across the barn windows. I don't think Grandma Gibson would be too happy if I brought them into the B&B, especially now it's the holiday season and it's nearly full of guests. My grandparents asked me and Dad to move into the house with them last night, so I think we'll be staying for good. I hope so. I've never seen Dad happier than when he's marching about with his hammer and nails fixing things around the farm.

"Did you miss me, Lady?" Adam asks. She winds herself round his legs like the answer's "yes" but then she goes running off as soon as she sees Grandma Gibson putting down a little bowl of leftover tuna flakes for her from the casserole. We both laugh at that. At least Bingo's loyal. He stays with me and doesn't even try to stick his nose in Lady's bowl cos he knows no matter how much she loves him, Lady loves her food even more.

"Can we go and see the cows after dinner?" Adam asks as we're taking our shoes off at the door. "They're up in the field past the B&B, aren't they?"

"Yeah, but they'll be taken back to the shed for milking soon, and that's even more fun to watch."

"Talking of things to watch..." Adam hesitates, like he wants to ask me something, but isn't sure if I'll say yes or not.

"What?"

"I was wondering...would you come and watch me swim in the competition? I mean, I know I won't win or anything, but it'd be great if you were there."

I give him my biggest banana-sunshine milkshake smile, and say, "Of course I will, Champ."

"Thanks, Sunny," he grins back.

I follow him into the farmhouse where I can hear his parents talking to my dad at the dinner table. Aunt Sandra's helping Grandma Gibson spoon out the casserole, and Grandpa Gibson's making sure everyone's got enough homemade lemonade. I stop in the doorway and just watch them for a bit, feeling a big bubble of happiness swelling up inside me till I'm so full I could burst.

I might not have a mum, but Adam's my best friend, and I've got Dad, Aunt Sandra, Grandma and Grandpa Gibson, a dog, a cat and her kittens, a herd of cows, eight pigs, five mice and three spiders, and that's more than enough for one person to love, isn't it?

ACKNOWLEDGEMENTS

As with every book, there are a huge number of people to thank for their support, and as always, my mother and my brother Martin are top of the list. My friends and family have been a wonderful source of encouragement, and I can't thank them enough for championing my novels.

A very big thank you goes to all of the wonderful teachers, librarians and pupils who have engaged with my books over the years. It's been amazing to visit so many schools and to see my novels being used to inspire class project work, group discussions, in-depth research into contemporary issues, artwork, drama classes, fan fiction, and so much more!

Special thanks go to the growing team at Neem Tree Press, whose enthusiasm and dedication has made them an absolute joy to work with. Writing can sometimes seem like a lonely business, but knowing I've got such a committed team working on my novels alongside me has meant the journey from first draft to publication has been supported every step of the way, for which I'm very grateful.

This particular book has provided the opportunity for me to research issues surrounding child poverty and homelessness, and to find out more about some of the housing organisations who work tirelessly to help families like Norah and her father. In order to support the great work they do in advocating on behalf of children growing up in temporary accommodation,

20% of the author royalties for this novel will be donated to Shelter.

ABOUT THE AUTHOR

Victoria Williamson is an award-winning children's author and primary school teacher from Scotland. She previously volunteered as a reading tutor with The Book Bus charity in Zambia and is now a Patron of Reading with CharChar Literacy to promote early years phonics teaching in Malawi. Victoria is passionate about creating inclusive worlds in her novels where all children can see themselves reflected.

Discover more books by Victoria Williamson:

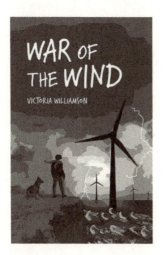
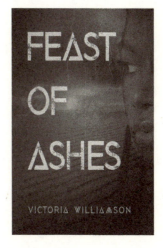